Pure and Untouched

BY

Barbara Cartland

New York   **EVEREST HOUSE**   *Publishers*

LIBRARY OF CONGRESS CATALOGING IN PUBLICATION DATA:

Cartland, Barbara, 1902 –
   Pure and untouched.
   I. Title.
PR6005.A765P8   *823'.912*   *81-3082*
ISBN: 0-89696-138-9   *AACR2*

AUTHOR'S NOTE

The fear engendered by the cruel, eccentric, tyrannical Nicholas I, 1825-1855, undoubtably the most alarming Sovereign who ever reigned, changed the lives of his fifty million subjects.

There was nothing with which he did not interfere and nobody was safe from his jurisdiction.

If the firebells rang in St. Petersburg, he ran out and told the firemen what to do about it. He banished Prince Yusupov to the Caucasus because he was having a love-affair of which his mother did not approve.

When the daughter of a Courtier was treated badly by her husband, he had the marriage annulled and wrote majestically: "This young person shall be considered a virgin."

The Tsar's Secret Police, known as The Third Section, were terrifying, merciless, and inescapable. All Russia lived under the shadow of fear which continued even after Nicholas's death.

PURE AND UNTOUCHED

Chapter One
1889

THE door of the Library opened and Mr. Matthews, Private Secretary and Comptroller to the Duke of Ravenstock, crossed the room quietly to where his employer was writing at a desk in the window.

He stood respectfully waiting to be noticed, and after several seconds the Duke raised his head to ask impatiently:

"What do you want, Matthews?"

"I thought I would inform Your Grace that a present has just arrived from Marlborough House from Their Royal Highnesses the Prince and Princess of Wales."

The Duke appeared momentarily interested.

"What is it?"

"A rose bowl, Your Grace."

The Duke groaned.

"Not another?"

"This is a very fine example, Your Grace, of early Georgian silver."

"That means another letter that I shall have to write personally."

"I am afraid so, Your Grace."

"Well, put it on the list and make it short. I do not intend to spend my honeymoon writing letters."

"I feel sure, Your Grace, that those who have to wait for your expressions of gratitude will understand the reason."

The Duke smiled, and it brought such an expression of charm to his face that Mr. Matthews thought it was understandable that so many women found the Duke irresistible.

Tall, broad-shouldered, and outstandingly handsome, he was not only the most attractive man in London but also the most raffish.

His exploits on the Turf, the stories of his escapades which when they reached the ears of the Queen at Windsor incurred her displeasure, and most of all the gossip about his innumerable love-affairs, lost nothing in the telling, being both printed in the more disreputable newspapers and passed in whispers from mouth to mouth from the Drawing-Rooms of Mayfair to the Parlours of Suburbia.

There was no doubt that the Duke was amused by his notoriety and paid no attention to his critics.

He played up the implication of his name by choosing black not only as the predominant colouring of his carriages but also as his racing-colours.

At every race-meeting, as the Duke's horse, which was almost invariably the favourite in its race, came galloping towards the winning-post, there would be shouts of: "Raven Black!" "Raven Black!" echoing down the course.

The Duke was known as a seducer of women who were only too eager to be seduced by him.

This was further evidence of what his detractors called his "shocking wickedness," but his friends called it his irresistible "fascination."

Now at last, when those who loved the Duke, including all his relations, had given up hope of his ever settling down and being married, he had fallen in love.

For years everybody had expected that his wife would be one of the few available beauties belonging to the exclusive circle in which he himself moved.

The likely candidates were almost invariably widows, because at the age of thirty-four it was not likely that the Duke would be interested in young girls, for the simple reason that he never met any.

The Prince of Wales had set the pace with love-affairs which included the beautiful Lily Langtry, and it was now

well known that he was head-over-heels in love with the
alluring Lady Brooke.

The Duke's love-affairs ran the gamut from the more
spectacular actresses to the Queen's Ladies-in-Waiting, and
each liaison surpassed the last in causing raised eye-brows
and disapproving exclamations.

The Duke, however, sailed serenely through life, finding
that he was easily bored with the women who surrendered
far too quickly, and making those who pursued him not
only frustrated but extremely unhappy.

"I like to be the hunter," he said to himself, but it appeared that few women were content to watch him pass by
without giving chase.

He had only to look at them with that quizzical question-
ing in his eyes for them to reach out their white hands to
touch him and, almost before he knew their names, to
throw their arms round his neck.

"What the devil have you got, Ravenstock," the Prince of
Wales had asked him once, "that I do not have?"

"Impertinence, Sir!" the Duke had replied.

The Prince had laughed uproariously.

"I believe that really is the answer!" he had said between
guffaws.

Even so, when the Duke's love-affairs seemed to be last-
ing a shorter and shorter time, and the lines on his face were
becoming a little more cynical, those amongst his friends
who were genuinely fond of him wondered what could be
done.

The answer to their question appeared in the shape of
Lady Cleodel Wick.

The Duke met her quite by chance when he was staying in
a house-party which included the Prince of Wales at Warwick Castle, which was not far from the Castle owned by the
Earl of Sedgewick.

The Earl and Countess and their daughter Lady Cleodel
had come over for dinner, and the Duke, who was sitting

next to the nineteen-year-old, found himself astounded by her beauty and fascinated in a way he had not experienced for many years.

Mourning had prevented Lady Cleodel from appearing before in the Social World, and now she was a year older than the other débutantes who were being presented at Court at the beginning of April.

The Duke knew that if he had ever before seen the golden-haired, blue-eyed beauty in the crowded Throne-Room at Buckingham Palace, he would have remembered her.

Looking at her now in the light of the silver candelabra on the table, he thought it would be impossible for any woman to be so lovely.

While her hair was the shining gold of a sovereign, it was extraordinary that her blue eyes should be fringed with dark lashes.

When he had enthused about them, she had explained that she owed them to some Irish ancestor.

When she spoke it was with a soft, hesitating little voice which he would have found extremely seductive if he had not realised how young and pure she was.

He talked to her all through the meal, to the palpable annoyance of the lady on his other side, and when the gentlemen joined the ladies in the Drawing-Room, he had gone straight to Lady Cleodel's side to say that he would call on her the following day.

She had not been fulsomely grateful as any other woman would have been. Instead she had said:

"I must ask Mama if we will be at home. We have many engagements in the afternoons, even though we are in the country."

The Duke had made certain that the Countess would receive him, and when he returned to London he had called at Sedgewick House, where he had found to his surprise that Lady Cleodel was not always readily available.

On several occasions, when she must have been aware that he was coming, she had gone out.

He had danced with her at every Ball they had both attended, but the Duke for the first time in his life had to wait his turn to partner Lady Cleodel, and one night, to his astonishment, he was unable to obtain a single dance, owing to the fact that her programme was already full.

When two weeks later he proposed and was accepted, he had found that even then she was elusive.

The kisses which other women had been all too eager to give him, even before he asked for them, he thought sometimes were not exactly refused by Lady Cleodel but were undoubtedly avoided.

The Duke seized every possible chance of being alone with his fiancée, but she always kept him at arm's length.

"No, no, you must not touch me," she said when he tried to take her in his arms. "You know Mama would not approve of our being alone together if she knew of it."

"Why should she know?" the Duke asked.

"If my hair was ruffled and my lips looked — kissed, she would be — angry with me!"

"But I want to kiss you," he insisted.

"I want it too," Cleodel said softly, glancing up at him from under her dark eye-lashes, "but Mama would be cross, and then she would prevent us from being alone again."

This was something new in the Duke's experience, and he had to be content, even while he mocked at his own self-control, with kissing Cleodel's fingers instead of her lips.

He told himself that because she was so young he must have both patience and understanding.

At the same time, the grace with which she moved, and the things she said in her soft little voice which told him how much he had to teach her about life and love, made him become more and more infatuated.

The Sedgewicks made no pretence about not being delighted at the prospect of having such a distinguished and wealthy son-in-law.

Although the Earl had a large Estate, he was not a rich man. But he had indeed expected, because of her beauty, that his daughter would marry well.

What he and his wife had not anticipated was that she would catch the most eligible bachelor in the County, whose social position ranked only just below that of a Royal Prince.

If the Sedgewicks were surprised, it was nothing compared to the astonishment of everybody else. But it was only the Duke's most intimate friend, Harry Carrington, who was brave enough to say so to the prospective bridegroom.

He had just returned from Scotland where he had been salmon-fishing on the Spey, and at first he had thought it must be a joke.

"You always told me you would remain a bachelor until you were on your last legs!" he had said to the Duke when he found him alone at Ravenstock House.

"That is what I fully intended," the Duke had replied, "until I met Cleodel."

"I have already been told that she is very beautiful," Harry said tentatively, "but at nineteen, how will she cope with you?"

"There will be nothing to cope with," the Duke replied.

He saw the smile of incredulity on his friend's face.

"I know I said that I would not marry, because not only did I think I would never find a woman who would not bore me after a short time, but also because I had no intention of having a wife who would be kissing my best friend as soon as my back was turned."

"Are you insulting me?" Harry asked.

"No, merely stating facts," the Duke said. "The wives of all my best friends have been eager for me to make love to them, and while I am not prepared to refuse the favours that come my way, I am not going to pretend to you that I think it is a particularly desirable way of living."

Harry stared at him as if he had taken leave of his senses.

"My dear Raven," he said at length, "I had no idea you felt like that."

The Duke's eyes twinkled.

"To be frank, it was not something that particularly worried me until I met Cleodel."

"Worried you?" Harry exclaimed. "When I think of all those gorgeous creatures . . . "

The Duke put up his hand.

"Spare me the reminiscences for, as you know, I never talk about my *affaires de coeur*."

"Which is a good thing," Harry agreed. "But tell me how Lady Cleodel is different."

"You will see for yourself," the Duke had said evasively.

When Harry met Cleodel later in the day, he had understood.

Besides being beautiful, her face had what he supposed was a look of purity, and she was certainly very different from the sophisticated, experienced women with whom the Duke had associated in the past.

As he watched them together he told himself that the Duke would be alert to protect her against the advances of other men like himself, and it would indeed be a case of the poacher turned game-keeper.

That would keep him out of mischief, Harry thought with satisfaction, and because he really had a deep affection for his friend he was delighted that he had found happiness.

Since there was no reason for a long engagement and the Sedgewicks were terrified that they might lose the Duke, the wedding was fixed for late in June, before the Season came to an end.

It had to take place after Royal Ascot since the Duke had several horses running at that meeting, and, because it would have been very inconvenient to have it in the country during the Season, it was decided that the ceremony should be held at St. George's Hanover Square.

Cleodel was so busy buying her trousseau that the Duke found it hard to see very much of her, but occasionally he asserted himself and, because he was in love, complained that he was being neglected.

"I have no wish to do anything so — unkind," Cleodel said gently, "but I must have gowns in which to look — beautiful for — you."

"Are you really buying them for me?" the Duke asked.

"But of course!" she replied. "Everybody has told me how fastidious you are, so I am very — afraid of — failing you."

"You are perfect just as you are," the Duke said, "and all I want is for us to be married so that I can take you away alone and tell you how lovely you are."

"That will be very — exciting."

"I will make you excited," the Duke said, "and it will be the most thrilling thing I have ever done in my life!"

He spoke with a sincerity in his voice that surprised himself.

Then he put his arms round Cleodel and kissed her very gently, for he was aware that if he was in the least passionate or demanding, she would be frightened.

On one occasion she had held him at arm's length, saying:

"Please — please — "

"I do not mean to frighten you, my darling," the Duke said quickly.

"It is not that I am really — frightened," Cleodel said, "But as I have never been — kissed before, I feel — almost as if you are making me your — captive, and I am no longer — myself."

"It is I who am the captive," the Duke said. "Forgive me, my sweet, and I will not be rough with you again."

He kissed her hands, turning them over to kiss their soft pink palms, and as he did so he thought that no woman could be more attractive and at the same time more difficult to capture.

The women who had loved him in the past had found his behaviour not only incomprehensible but infuriating.

"Raven is the most fascinating devil who ever stalked London," one of them said, "but in the guise of a Saint I find him depressing."

"I agree with you," another of the Duke's loves said, "but make no mistake, that chit straight out of the School-Room will have lost him before Christmas."

"I am willing to wager that it will not last even as long as that," was the spiteful reply.

Strangely enough, the only person who did not admire Cleodel was Harry, but he was far too tactful to say anything to the Duke or to his other friends, who he was certain would repeat any criticism he made about the future Duchess.

But to himself he thought there was something about her that was not entirely natural.

He could not put his finger on it, but with her innocent little ways it was as if she was really too good to be true.

The Duke, however, was carried away on the wings of bliss, counting the hours until he could see his future bride again like any boy with his first love.

Because Ravenstock House in Park Lane was so much larger than the house the Earl owned in Green Street, it was decided that the Reception should be held in the former, and the Duke with his usual passion for perfection was organising every detail.

The guests were to be received in the Ball-Room which opened out into the garden.

The presents were to be displayed in the Picture-Gallery, and the Duke planned that the whole house should be decorated with flowers brought from his country Estate and arranged by his own gardeners.

It would be impossible to accommodate in London all his Estate workers, tenants, and farmers, and he therefore gave orders that only the heads of each department should sit in the Gallery of St. George's.

In the country, a huge marquee was to be erected on the lawn where all the others would start their celebrations late in the afternoon.

This meant that if after the Reception the Duke and his wife travelled from Park Lane straight to Ravenstock by his private train, they would arrive in time to receive their congratulations and good wishes.

He would make a short speech thanking them, after which there would be an enormous display of fireworks.

The bride and bridegroom would have to spend the first night of their honeymoon at Ravenstock, but to the Duke it was somehow very fitting that he should take his bride home on their wedding-night to the house of his ancestors.

It had never troubled him before that he had not an heir to succeed him, but now he told himself that nothing could be better or more perfect than that his son should be born to two people who loved each other as he and Cleodel did.

"Tell me you love me," he had said to her insistently the previous evening as they sat in the garden of Devonshire House, where they were attending a Ball.

"I have — given you my — heart," Cleodel replied.

"It is something which I shall treasure forever!"

He had even contemplated writing a poem to her, but instead he was writing her a letter extolling her perfections, which he intended to send round to Sedgewick House with a large bouquet of lilies-of-the-valley.

He thought that that particular flower best typified her with its delicacy and its fragrance, and there was something very young about it, because it never became full-blown like a rose.

He was just finishing his letter when Mr. Matthews appeared again.

"What is it now, Matthews?" the Duke asked.

"I am sorry to disturb Your Grace again," Mr. Matthews replied, "but the Dowager Countess of Glastonbury has arrived, and I know you will wish to see Her Ladyship."

The Duke rose from the desk immediately.

"Of course! But I had no idea my grandmother was coming to London."

Leaving the letter unfinished, he walked from the Library to the Drawing-Room, where his maternal grandmother was waiting to see him.

Now in her eighties, the Dowager Countess still held herself as straight as a ramrod, and it was impossible not to realise that she had been a great beauty in her youth.

Her hair was dead white, her face was lined, but her features were classical and had remained unchanged.

When the Duke appeared she held out her hands with a little cry of delight.

"Grandmama!" the Duke exclaimed. "I had no idea that you were well enough to come to London. Why did you not let me know?"

"I did not make up my mind until the last moment," the Dowager Countess replied. "But when I had an invitation from the Queen to stay at Windsor, for the races at Ascot, I could not resist accepting it."

The Duke, having kissed her cheek, sat down beside her, holding one of her hands in his.

He looked at her with laughter in his eyes. Then he said:

"That is a very lame excuse, Grandmama! I have a feeling that the real reason why you have come to London is to look at my future wife."

The Dowager chuckled.

"I confess that is the truth! I could not believe that any young girl would catch 'Casanova' after he had resisted every bait and hook cast over him for so many years!"

"I was a very willing catch."

"That is what is impossible to believe!" the Dowager Countess flashed.

The Duke laughed.

"Let me say, Grandmama, how delighted I am that you are here, and of course you are staying with me."

"Of course!" she replied. "I do not know of anybody else with such an attentive staff or another house that is as comfortable as this."

"I am flattered."

The Dowager Countess looked at him with her eyes that were still shrewd despite her age.

"Is it true that you have definitely lost your heart?" she asked.

The Duke smiled.

"Wait until you see Cleodel, then you will understand."

"I doubt it," the Dowager Countess said, "and I think, like all the other women you have loved, I am going to miss the Buccaneer who was invincible and the Pirate who invariably captured the prize."

The Duke's laughter rang out.

"Grandmama, you are priceless! Nobody else ever talks to me as you do, and in such amusing language. But this Pirate has struck his flag, and now I am going to settle down to domesticity."

"Fiddlesticks!" the Dowager Countess declared. "And you will certainly have to find something to take the place of the women in your life."

"That will be Cleodel," the Duke said.

The Dowager Countess did not reply, because at that moment servants came in carrying the tea.

By the time they had set the table with silver and produced every form of delicacy to eat, the Duke was talking not of himself but of the presents they had received and the places they were to visit on their honeymoon.

His grandmother listened attentively, and she thought, as Harry had done, that it seemed incredible that after all the glamorous, brilliant, spectacular women who had attracted him, the Duke should have succumbed to the fascination of a young girl who, however lovely, had nothing much to offer him except youth.

If he had been much older, the Dowager Countess thought to herself, she would have been able to say "there is no fool like an old fool," but the Duke was still young, except perhaps by comparison with the girl he was to marry.

Then she told herself that all that mattered was that he was happy.

She had always loved "Raven," as he had been called since he was a very small boy, more than her other grandchildren.

It was his naughtiness which had started almost from the time he was in the cradle that had amused her, and, having herself been brought up in the Regency period, she found the prim solemnity of the Victorians extremely boring.

She had always thought that the Duke would have felt far more at home with George IV, and when she heard him criticised she excused him for bringing amusement and a sense of adventure to an age that was not only prudish but hypocritical in its outlook.

One of her other grandchildren had told her that he was shocked at his cousin's way of life and his innumerable love-affairs, but the Dowager Countess had merely looked him up and down and said contemptuously:

"The trouble with you is that you are jealous! If you had the looks or the guts to behave like Raven, you would do so! As it is, you can only grind your teeth and wish you were in his shoes."

Because the Duke had so much to say to his grandmother he did not leave her until she retired to her own room, and because they had been talking until the last moment he had to dress in a hurry.

He was dining at Marlborough House, and it was only as he was going downstairs, resplendent in knee-breeches and wearing his decorations on his evening-coat, that he remembered he had not finished his letter to Cleodel.

It had been left in the Library with his bouquet of lilies-of-the-valley, which he had intended to send with it.

Quickly he hurried to his desk, added to the letter a last expression of his love, and put it in an envelope.

Then as he picked up the bouquet, which he intended to tell his coachman to leave for Cleodel after taking him to Marlborough House, a thought came to him.

It brought a smile to his lips and he wondered why he had not thought of it before.

*

Carrying the lilies-of-the-valley, the Duke stepped into his carriage, and as he turned towards Marlborough House he was thinking of Cleodel and how he had been unable to see her all day.

Yesterday they had met for a brief drive in the Park, then again at a Ball, but on neither of those occasions had he been able to kiss her.

He found himself yearning for her with an intensity which actually surprised him.

He had kissed so many women and had always felt that one kiss was very much like another, but with Cleodel it was different.

He thought perhaps it was because as she was so young and so innocent she never completely surrendered herself to him.

Because she was unawakened and perhaps a little fearful, there was always a barrier between them.

It was a barrier which he had every intention of removing as soon as they were married, and again he thought how thrilling it would be to awaken her to womanhood.

"I want her! God knows I want her!" he told himself, and he was still thinking of her as the carriage drew up at Marlborough House.

As he alighted he said to his footman:

"I have left some flowers and a note in the carriage. Do not touch them, but come back in three hours' time."

"Very good, Your Grace."

The Duke was greeted by the Prince of Wales and several of his friends, and a number of beautiful women who in the past had aroused his interest for a short time.

As always, the party at Marlborough House was amusing and the conversation glittered and sparkled like a jewel in a crown.

The Duke had one of his "old flames" sitting beside him at dinner, and almost immediately the meal started she asked:

"Is it true, Raven, that you are a reformed character and that your horns are turning white?"

"Will it surprise you if I tell you the answer is 'yes'?" the Duke replied.

"I have always heard that 'a leopard never changes his spots'!"

"You have your metaphors a little mixed, Kitty," the Duke said with a smile, "and in this instance you are wrong."

"Nonsense, Raven! And think how bored we shall all be if you take to psalm-singing and supporting waifs and strays."

The Duke laughed before he replied:

"In the past I have usually been accused of contributing to the latter!"

"That would not surprise me," Kitty remarked, "and it would certainly be in character."

"Now you are being unkind!" the Duke protested. "As far as I know, I have no love-children on my conscience."

"I am sure that is wishful thinking," Kitty said. "And what has this paragon to whom you are engaged got that we who have loved you for years have not?"

"Cleodel is the most adorable person I have ever known."

Kitty groaned.

"That is no consolation when another woman has succeeded where I have failed."

They sparred until the meal was over, then because the Princess was present there was no gambling and before midnight the guests began to leave.

"Are you going to win the Gold Cup, Raven?" the Prince asked as the Duke said good night.

"I hope so, Sir."

"Dammit! That means that my own horse has no chance," the Prince grumbled.

"It is always a question of luck."

"And yours has never failed you yet, so if you meant to console me there is no point in my listening to you."

Then, because the Prince of Wales was in fact very fond of the Duke, he put his arm through his and walked with him towards the door saying:

"When you are married, Raven, I cannot lose you, and I want you and your wife to stay at Sandringham for my first shoot."

"We shall be very honoured, Sir."

"Which means that you will mark up the biggest bag," the Prince said. "I am a fool to ask you."

"I will do my best not to be obtrusive, Sir," the Duke said humbly.

But both men laughed, knowing that such a thing where the Duke was concerned was impossible.

He left Marlborough House and told his coachman to carry him to Green Street.

When the carriage stopped, he got out, carrying the lilies-of-the-valley and the note for Cleodel.

"Go home," he said to the footman. "I will walk from here."

The man was at first surprised, then amused, but many years of training prevented him from showing what he felt, and he managed to keep his expression impersonal until he was back on the box and the horses were moving away.

The Duke waited until his conveyance was out of sight,

then he walked down a mews which brought him to the back of Sedgewick House.

He knew that behind the houses on Green Street there was quite a large garden, in which he had often sat out when there were dances and invariably kissed his partners in discreet little arbours or in the shelter of a leafy tree.

There was a door from the garden into the mews, but this was locked and each householder kept a key to it.

The Duke was extremely athletic, and the exercise he took riding, fencing, and boxing kept him in the peak of condition.

Despite being slightly constricted by his tight-fitting evening-coat, he swung himself lithely up onto the top of the wall which bordered the mews and dropped down on the other side.

He thought with satisfaction that he had not even laddered his silk stockings in doing so, and now he moved through the shrubs that hid this part of the garden from the green lawn and Sedgewick House directly ahead of him.

It was the last house on the street and rather different from the others, being older and more rambling.

On the ground floor was a Dining-Room, a rather ugly, elongated room, an attractive Drawing-Room with three French windows which opened onto the garden, and beyond that the small Sitting-Room where he had sometimes been allowed to be alone with Cleodel.

Above this was her bedroom, with a balcony that was matched by one at the other end of the house, where her mother slept.

The Duke had actually teased her about the balcony, saying that one night like Romeo he would serenade her from the garden.

Cleodel had looked at him apprehensively.

"If you did — that," she had said, "Mama would hear you and she would think it was an — extremely improper — way to — behave!"

"Perhaps," the Duke had agreed, "but it would be very romantic, my darling, and that is what you make me feel."

Cleodel had looked up at him from under her long eye-lashes.

"I like you to be romantic," she had said, "like a Knight in a fairy-story who fights a dragon for me."

"Of course," the Duke had agreed, "and you know I would slay all the dragons, however ferocious they might be."

"That is how I want you to feel," Cleodel had said softly.

The Duke thought now that it would seem very romantic to Cleodel when tomorrow morning she found the bouquet of lilies-of-the-vally and his note on her balcony.

He knew from the way the house was built that he would not find it difficult to climb up the wall of the Sitting-Room and pull himself up onto the balcony so that he could leave the flowers where he wished them to be.

He thought it would be difficult for any woman not to appreciate the trouble he had taken to please her, and he knew that if he had done anything like this in the past, the lady in question would not only have been thrilled by his attention but would undoubtedly have invited him in.

He found himself wondering if it would be too outra-geous if, having reached the balcony, he called and awakened Cleodel, who would be asleep.

He was certain that any apprehension she had about her mother overhearing them was unnecessary.

The Countess was slightly deaf and the two bedrooms were separated by the whole width of the house, so that even if he shouted at Cleodel her mother would be unlikely to hear him.

The Duke walked through the shrubs holding his bouquet carefully, and by the light of the stars and a young moon climbing up the sky he saw the house ahead clearly.

Then he stopped dead.

For a moment he thought it must be an illusion, a trick of the light.

But he soon saw unmistakably that there was a man climbing up a ladder which was propped against the side of the balcony.

The top of the ladder just reached the bottom of the stone balustrade with which the balcony was surrounded.

Because of the way it was placed, the man was sideways to the Duke and slightly in shadow.

He supposed it was a burglar who intended to rob Cleodel, and it flashed through his mind that nothing could be more fortunate than that he should have come here at this very moment to prevent such an outrage.

Moreover, it would give him the opportunity of proving that he was in fact a Knight protecting the woman he loved against a very unpleasant dragon.

Then as he quietly moved forward he became aware that the burglar was in evening-dress, which seemed strange, and as the man reached the top of the ladder and pulled himself up onto the stone balustrade, the Duke could see his face.

Once again he stopped abruptly, unable to believe his eyes.

The man whom he'd thought was a burglar was in fact a friend, a member of his Club, and only last evening when they were having a drink together Jimmy Hudson had lifted his glass.

"Good luck, Raven!" he had said. "May you always be as successful as you are today!"

The Duke had thanked him, and now as he watched Jimmy throwing his leg over the balcony he felt he must be dreaming.

Then through the bedroom window came somebody in white.

It was Cleodel, and the Duke was sure that she would be appalled and shocked by Jimmy's intrusion.

He waited for her to scream, then decided that he would appear and tell Jimmy what he thought of him and make him sorry he had ever attempted to do anything so outrageous.

Then as the Duke planned to climb the ladder to confront Jimmy unless he retreated at once before Cleodel's wrath, he saw that they were suddenly and unexpectedly clasped in each other's arms.

Cleodel's face was lifted to Jimmy's and he was kissing her, kissing her passionately in a way that the Duke had been unable to do himself, because of her protests and because he was afraid of frightening her.

Their kiss took a long time, while the Duke stood as if turned to stone, unable to breathe.

Then almost reluctantly, as it seemed to him, Cleodel moved from Jimmy's arms and put out her hand to draw him into the darkness of her bedroom.

As she did so she smiled, and the moonlight seemed to light her face with a sudden radiance which made her appear even more beautiful than he had ever seen her before.

Then the balcony was empty, and there was only the ladder standing at one side of it, to make the Duke quite certain of what he had seen and what she had done.

Chapter Two

FOR what seemed to him a very long time, though it could have been only a few minutes, the Duke stood staring at the empty balcony, and as he did so, like a puzzle falling into place he saw how he had been deceived and tricked.

The Duke was not only extremely intelligent, but he had a very retentive memory.

It had stood him in good stead both at Eton and at Oxford, where he had found that by doing only the minimum amount of work he could win prizes and awards.

Now seeing his past flash before his eyes as if through a magic lantern, he saw Jimmy Hudson telling him when they were staying at Warwick Castle that the Earl of Sedgewick had good horses and he was borrowing one to ride in the local Steeple-Chase.

"Be a good friend, Raven, and do not enter for it," he had begged. "I want to win."

The Duke had smiled.

"What is the prize?" he had enquired.

"One thousand pounds, a Silver Cup, and a pulsating young heart," Jimmy had replied blithely.

The Duke had laughed and agreed not to enter the Steeple-Chase, knowing that while the "pulsating young heart" might be an allurement, the thousand pounds was far more important to Jimmy.

Jimmy Hudson, with whom he had been at Eton, was the son of a country Squire who had a Manor House and a very small Estate in the Shires.

On leaving School, when the Duke went to Oxford, Jimmy had served for four years in the Brigade of Guards, and then had realised he could not afford to stay in the Regiment, nor was it getting him anywhere.

He decided that if he was to live the life he enjoyed, the only possible thing for him to do was to marry an heiress.

He contrived to get an introduction to one of London's most renowned hostesses who had two rather plain but definitely rich daughters.

What James Hudson had done was to underrate his own attractions.

He was extremely good-looking in the rather conventional English manner, and he had, when he wished to use it, a charm which, combined with good manners, women found very attractive.

It was not the daughters who were attracted to him in this particular house, but the mother!

After he had squired her from party to party and was invited to her very exclusive house-parties in the country where the guests included the Prince of Wales, Jimmy found a place in Society to which even in his wildest flights of imagination he had never aspired.

Because he was prepared to make himself pleasant not only to attractive women but to everybody else, and also because he was a good card-player, an excellent rider, and an amusing raconteur of after-dinner stories, he became one of the Marlborough House Set.

The Prince of Wales had extended the boundaries of Society to include any man or woman who amused him, and as Jimmy definitely kept him laughing, hostesses soon realised his worth. As the invitations piled up on the mantelpiece in his lodgings, he often complained of how little time he had to answer them.

His winnings at cards paid some of his tailor's bills and provided him with enough money to tip the servants in the houses in which he stayed. But everything else he desired was free.

The ladies who found him a compelling and ardent lover

provided him with gold cuff-links and a great many other
luxuries that could certainly not be furnished from his
meagre Bank-balance.

Like the Duke until he had met Cleodel, Jimmy had had
no intention of becoming a married man.

To be confined to one woman when he could find a
welcome in almost every Mayfair *Boudoir* would be unpleasantly restrictive when he was riding on the crest of the social
wave in a manner which amazed not only his friends but
himself.

Thinking back, the Duke knew that it must have been
before he had arranged to ride the Earl of Sedgewick's
horses to compete in the Steeple-Chase that Jimmy had met
Cleodel.

It would have been unlike Jimmy's usual technique to pay
any attention to such a young girl, but Cleodel, as the Duke
was well aware, was different, and the year which she had
lost in mourning would have made her eager for excitement.

It would, he thought savagely, have been Jimmy who had
taught her how to attract and capture the most glittering
social *parti* in the whole country.

He had often discussed with Jimmy the way women made
the love-affairs in which they both indulged far too easy,
and in doing so they eliminated the thrill of the chase and
the excitement of being the victor in what had been a
difficult contest.

The Duke never mentioned any woman by name or indicated that he was talking of anybody in whom he was or had
been particularly interested, but generalising he had said to
Jimmy:

"Dammit all, I like a run for my money!"

He remembered now how Jimmy had agreed with him,
saying:

"I often feel I am a fox with the whole pack of hounds
after me and the field thundering behind."

They both had laughed.

Other conversations they had had on much the same theme were now coming back to the Duke.

He could see, almost as if it were a picture forming in front of his eyes, how Jimmy had understood exactly what he was wanting and what would be alluring because it was a new experience.

When Cleodel had held off his advances and had never seemed over-eager to see him again, and the times when he had felt frustrated by her indifference and her refusal to dance with him, it had all been a challenge which he had found irresistible.

He thought it must have been Jimmy who had told her even when they were engaged to keep him almost at arm's length, although of course he now suspected that she was in love with Jimmy and found no other man as desirable as he.

The fact that he had been humiliated and made a fool of made the Duke want to climb the ladder and confront Cleodel and Jimmy in a way which would leave them embarrassed and ashamed.

Then he told himself that that would be too easy a revenge. Moreover, it would spark off an almighty row, and since he did not want the whole world to learn how he had been cuckolded by one of his closest friends, it seemed he must go on with the marriage and make Cleodel his wife.

Then the Duke's lips set in a hard line, and he told himself that he would be damned if he would marry any woman who was behaving as Cleodel was at this moment. The mere thought of it made him so angry that he seemed to see the whole house and especially the balcony crimson as if with blood.

Then has he took an impulsive step forward, he told himself that he must be more subtle and hurt Cleodel and Jimmy as they had hurt him.

A plan came to his mind and he turned slowly and walked

back to the door which led from the garden into a side-
street.

As he expected, it was possible to open it from the inside,
and he let himself out and started to walk slowly down the
deserted road.

It was only as he came to a dust-bin that he was aware that
he was still holding the bouquet of lilies-of-the-valley and
the letter he had written to Cleodel telling her how much he
loved her.

He stared at both things as if he had never seen them
before.

Then slowly and deliberately he crushed the delicate
flowers into a pulp before he flung them into the bin, and
tore the letter he had written with its passionate expressions
of love into small pieces and scattered them over the gar-
bage.

As he walked on, his face was set in hard, cynical lines that
made him look much older than his years.

*

The Duke crossed the Channel the following morning in
his yacht, which was always kept in Dover harbour, ready to
sail at an hour's notice.

Because a Courier had arrived long before the Duke, the
Captain could actually weigh anchor immediately after His
Grace had come aboard.

The efficiency which the Duke expected from his staff
and which resulted in the almost perfect organisation of his
houses and Estates had been put to the test when, on arriv-
ing back at Ravenstock House after midnight, he had sent
for Mr. Matthews.

The night-footman had hurried upstairs and in under
ten minutes Mr. Matthews, conventionally dressed, had
joined his employer in the Library.

The Duke's orders were given sharply and briefly, with

the result that a number of the servants spent most of the night packing, a Courier left for Dover at dawn, and the Duke's private railway-carriage was attached to one of the early trains leaving for Dover.

Having issued his commands like a General going into battle, the Duke had then retired to his own bedroom.

The next morning he appeared downstairs for breakfast dressed elegantly but with, his servants thought apprehensively, a scowl on his face which they had not seen since he had fallen in love.

When Mr. Matthews handed the Duke his passport and a very large sum of money, he said quietly:

"May I ask, Your Grace, what I am to say to any enquirers as to your whereabouts?"

"After you have sent the notice to *The Gazette, The Times*, and *The Morning Post*, as I instructed you," the Duke replied coldly, "stating that my marriage to Lady Cleodel has been postponed, you will have nothing else to impart."

"Nothing, Your Grace?" Mr. Matthews asked nervously.

"Nothing!" the Duke answered firmly.

"If Lady Cleodel and the Earl . . . " Mr. Matthews began.

"You heard what I said, Matthews!" the Duke interrupted.

"Very good, Your Grace, I will carry out your orders and see that everybody else in the house does the same."

The Duke did not reply. He merely walked away to step into the closed carriage that was waiting to convey him to the station.

The Channel-crossing was smooth. His Courier met him at Dover and he was escorted by several high-ranking railway-officials to a private carriage which had been attached to the Express to Paris.

His house in the Champs Élysées was ready for his arrival, and the next morning a carriage driven by four finely bred horses was ready to take him out of Paris on a road which led in the direction of Versailles.

The Duke, however, did not intend to look at the residence of forgotten Kings. Instead he went to a small village, where his horses stopped outside the Convent of the *Sacré-Coeur*.

Anybody who knew the Duke would have thought it a strange place for him to call. Yet, once again he was expected, and a smiling Nun opened the iron-studded door and led him through cool, cloister-like passages to a room overlooking the Convent garden, through the windows of which the sun was shining in a golden haze.

"His Grace *le Duc,* Reverend Mother!" the Nun said as she opened the door.

A woman in white, writing at a desk in the window, rose to her feet with a little cry of gladness.

She held out her hands and the Duke took them in his and bent his head to kiss her cheek.

"How are you, Marguerite?" he asked.

"It is delightful to see you, Raven dear," she replied, "but it is a great surprise. I thought you would be far too busy in London to visit Paris, unless it was on your honeymoon."

As she spoke, she saw that her brother's eyes darkened and a scowl disfigured his handsome face.

Perceptive as she had always been, Lady Marguerite said quickly:

"What is wrong? What has happened?"

"That is what I have come to talk to you about," the Duke replied. "Shall we sit down?"

"Of course. I have ordered you some wine and some of the little biscuits that you remember are a specialty of my Convent."

The Duke smiled, but there was no need for a reply, for as the Reverend Mother spoke, a Nun came in through the door with the wine and biscuits on a tray.

She set them down beside the sofa, made a respectful curtsey, then left the room.

The Duke looked at his sister.

Although she was fifteen years older than he, he thought she still looked a young woman and had not lost the beauty that had made her so outstanding when she had made her début.

The late Duke of Ravenstock and his wife had been confident that their only daughter, Marguerite, would make a brilliant Society marriage.

The Ball they had given at Ravenstock House had been attended not only by every eligible young aristocrat in the whole of *Debrett,* but also by a large number of younger sons of reigning Monarchs and foreign Princes.

It was not quite what they had expected but at the same time it was acceptable when Lady Marguerite had fallen in love with the elder son of Lord Lansdown.

He was somewhat older than she was, had made a name for himself in the Army, and was a serious, rather unsociable character. His name had never been connected with any woman and he was in fact known to be dedicated to his Regiment.

The moment he saw Lady Marguerite he had known she was the one woman who had ever mattered to him and he had lost his heart irretrievably.

The Duke and Duchess had agreed to the marriage and it was arranged that it should take place in six months' time.

Marguerite, because she felt as if she were walking in the sunshine of Paradise, was prepared to do anything that was asked of her as long as eventually she could marry the man she loved.

They were together every moment that Arthur Lansdown could get away from his Regimental duties. Then, two months before they were due to be married, he was sent abroad on a special mission to the Sudan where there was a rumour of trouble amongst the tribes.

Since no hostilities had broken out, there was not the slightest expectation of his being in any danger. But he was assassinated by the knife of a tribesman who was intent on a revenge which existed only in his own distorted mind.

For Marguerite, her world came to an end. She would not listen to anything anybody said to her, nor would she accept any form of consolation from her family.

Because she could not bear to be in any place where she had been with Arthur, she left England despite every protest and entered a Convent in France.

She was accepted into the Catholic Church, and although her father and mother pleaded with her almost on their knees to give herself time to recover from her bereavement, she would not listen to them.

She eventually took the veil irrevocably when she had not yet reached her twenty-first birthday.

Because she was extremely intelligent and also very rich, as the years passed she rose from being an ordinary Nun to having what was to all intents and purposes her own Convent on the outskirts of Paris.

It housed a number of Nuns who came from families of equal importance to that of her father, and also Novices who the Church thought should consider and think before they finally vowed away their freedom to spend their lives in prayer and chastity.

Lady Marguerite won the approval not only of her Cardinal in France but also of the Pope and officials of the Vatican in Rome.

The Duke could understand that in her own way she provided a service that was unique within the Church, giving those who were as intelligent and as well-born as herself a chance to serve God and at the same time not to waste their talents.

Some of the Nuns under his sister had written books which had been acclaimed in the outside world, while the embroidery and the lace that came from the Convent of the *Sacré-Coeur* evoked the admiration of everybody who saw it.

Every time the Duke visited his sister he realised that despite the fact that the Social World thought she had wasted her life, Marguerite was in fact a very happy woman and entirely self-sufficient.

What was more, her vocation had given her a sympathy and an understanding which made him know that he could turn to her in any emergency in his own life, and that was why he was here now.

Lady Marguerite poured out the wine for him, then seated herself beside him to ask gently:

"What has happened, Raven?"

"I do not want to talk about it," her brother replied harshly. "But I want you to find me a wife who is pure and untouched!"

If he had meant to startle his sister, he certainly succeeded.

But Lady Marguerite did not exclaim or in fact say anything. She only looked at him with an expression of surprise in her blue eyes, which then turned to one of compassion.

"Why have you come to me, Raven?" she enquired after a long pause.

"Because I know that only here amongst your young women who think they may have a vocation will I find a girl who has not been contaminated by the world — or should I say by other men?"

There was no escaping the bitterness in his voice, which told Lady Marguerite without explanation what had happened.

She clasped her hands in her lap and looked away from her brother before she said:

"If ever I doubted the efficacy of prayer; you have now convinced me that it is always answered."

The Duke did not speak. He merely waited for her to go on, and finally his sister continued:

"I have been praying about a certain problem for some time, and now, when I least expected it, when I felt the answer lay in a different direction altogether, you are here."

"You can give me what I have asked you for?" the Duke enquired.

His sister gave a sigh.

"I could do so. At the same time, I am afraid. I question whether it is something I should do."

The Duke's lips twisted as if he knew what she was thinking, and after a moment he said:

"Suppose you explain to me in so many words what you are thinking and the reason for your prayers?"

As if she was shaken out of her habitual serenity, Lady Marguerite rose and walked towards the window.

She stood looking out on the sunlit formal garden, and on the green lawns she could see some of her young Nuns wearing white habits that she had designed to seem less austere and certainly less ugly than those worn in most Convents.

The veils of the Novices were white and transparent, and instead of the heavy leather shoes that were habitual to other Nuns, those in the Convent of the *Sacré-Coeur* wore light slippers so that they moved more gracefully.

The Duke waited, and after a little while, as if she had made up her mind to tell him what she was thinking, his sister turned from the window.

"Eight years ago," she began, sitting down again in the chair she had recently vacated, "a child was left outside the gates of the Convent. She arrived in a carriage, and after those who had conveyed her here had rung the bell, they immediately drove away. A Nun opened the door and brought her to me. She carried in her hand an envelope which contained the sum of five thousand pounds and a few words written on a piece of paper."

"Five thousand pounds!" the Duke exclaimed.

"It was a very large sum," his sister said, "and the letter, which I will show you, said:

"This is Anoushka. Her father is English and wishes you to bring her up. She is, however, not to take the veil until she is over twenty-one, and then only if it is her wish to do so. Money will be provided for her to have the best teachers available."

Lady Marguerite ceased speaking and the Duke asked:

"Was that all? There was no signature?"

"No, nothing. The writing was educated, and I think it was that of an Englishman."

The Duke raised his eye-brows and his sister gave a little laugh.

"I was guessing, just as I have guessed all through the years, but I have come to no conclusion."

"How many years?" the Duke asked.

"Anoushka is now nearly eighteen, and my problem is what I should do with her."

"You do not intend to keep her until she is twenty-one and let her become a Nun?"

"No."

"Why not?"

"For two reasons. First, because I do not think she is suited for the confined life. She is brilliantly intelligent, extremely talented in many ways, and has a strange character which I find hard to understand."

Lady Marguerite paused, and the Duke said:

"And the other reason?"

"Two years ago I received the sum of seventy thousand pounds. Since then there has been no more."

"There had been some previously?"

"Yes. Every two years after her arrival I received another five thousand pounds. Of course I have not spent it all, but with seventy thousand pounds Anoushka is a very wealthy young woman."

"So what do you intend to do with her?"

"That was my problem, and I was seriously considering whether to approach one of our relatives to ask her to introduce the girl to Society and let her see the world outside these Convent walls."

Lady Marguerite gave her brother an almost pleading glance as she said:

"I have prayed and prayed for what was best to do, and now you are here."

"It does indeed seem obvious that I am the answer to your problem and your prayers," the Duke said.

Lady Marguerite did not have to speak.

"But you are thinking of my reputation," the Duke went on, "and of course that I have recently announced my engagement to another woman. Let me make this clear — that engagement no longer exists."

Lady Marguerite was still silent, and the Duke continued:

"As for my reputation, the family, as you well know, have been pleading with me for years to have an heir. That is what I now intend to do, but my wife must be, as I have already said, pure and untouched. I will not tolerate the woman who shall bear my name being anything else."

Again there was a note in the Duke's voice which told his sister very clearly what had happened.

"I cannot imagine Anoushka being married to somebody like you!" she said after a moment. "I hoped that perhaps she would find a man who would love her and whom she would love, but I was well aware that one of the difficulties would be that she has no name."

The Duke gave a slight shrug of his shoulders.

"Is that important?"

"Socially, it would certainly raise a difficult problem."

"Whoever she might be," the Duke said, "there would be few people brave enough to question my wife's antecedents if I did not wish to speak of them."

Lady Marguerite knew this was true, and she said:

"We also have to think of the family, Raven. Although I am absolutely convinced that Anoushka is an aristocrat in every sense of the word and that her blood is as blue as ours, we have to face the fact that she may be a love-child."

"So have been many who have adorned history, especially in France," the Duke said.

Lady Marguerite gave a little sigh.

"I feel as if I am dealing with a problem which is too big for me," she said. "How could I have guessed, how could I have anticipated for a moment when I was praying about Anoushka's future that it could be linked with yours?"

She looked at her brother pleadingly as she said:

"Am I doing the right thing, Raven? Or have you talked me into it? Perhpas I am wrong in even considering a life for her outside these walls. At the same time, my experience here has taught me to know when an enclosed life is right for a young girl, or whether she should live in a very different way and above all know the happiness of having a husband and — children."

There was just a little tremor as Lady Marguerite said the last word, which told the Duke, if he had not known it already, that she still was faithful to the memory of the man to whom she had been engaged.

Having known what had seemed a perfect and complete love, she would never forget it.

"I think, Marguerite," the Duke said, "you have answered your own questions, and where this girl is concerned you can trust to your instinct, which often gives far better guidance than the logic offered us by our brains."

Lady Marguerite smiled.

"Thank you, Raven. That is very complimentary, and I like to think you are right. My instinct tells me that Anoushka belongs to a far broader world than I can offer her. At the same time, you must realise that she knows nothing of the life you lead and which you take as a matter of course."

Suddenly Lady Marguerite got up from her chair to say:

"Here we are talking as if something has been decided

between us. I have been hypnotised by what you have asked and am no longer thinking straight. How can you possibly marry a girl you have never seen and who has never seen you?"

"Now you are listening to your mind and not your instinct," the Duke said. "You know as well as I do that in many Eastern countries the bride and bridgroom seldom see each other before the actual wedding-day, and even if we had met, I doubt if the girl in question or those concerned with her, which in this case is yourself, would turn down the chance of her becoming a Duchess."

"That is very cynical, Raven."

"But practical," the Duke replied.

"I still cannot think why, after you have walked in here with such a ridiculous propositon, we have sat down and talked it over as if it were quite a usual thing to happen."

"It may be unusual but it is not ridiculous," the Duke said, "and just as I have turned to you for help, so you are prepared to give me exactly what I have asked for."

"Wait!" Lady Marguerite said. "You are going too quickly. First you must meet Anoushka. Then you must decide how you can marry a young woman without a name and without the family being horrified because they have not been consulted."

"Let me make this absolutely clear. As regards my marriage I will consult no-one!" the Duke replied. "I am not concerned with the family or with anybody else. I intend to be married immediately. I have no wish to explain my reasons to you or to anybody else. Let me simply say that this is something I intend to do, and nobody shall prevent me!"

There was something so positive in the Duke's voice and another note in it that made Lady Marguerite look at him apprehensively.

For the first time in all the years she had known him, she thought that her brother looked not only grim but cruel.

There was an expression in his eyes which she had never seen before, and it made her say quickly:

"Whatever has hurt you, Raven, do not let it spoil you. You have done many things of which it is impossible not to disapprove, but you have always been kind and generous and because you have been happy you have given happiness to other people."

She put out her hand and laid it on her brother's arm.

"I know you are suffering," she said gently, "but those who are innocent of any crime towards you must not suffer too."

"I do not know what you are talking about," the Duke said defensively.

"I think you do," Lady Marguerite answered, "and remember, hatred is a boomerang which always eventually hurts oneself."

"I am not admitting I hate anybody," the Duke said. "I am only avenging an insult in a way which will be extremely effective."

"You will make somebody unhappy?"

"I sincerely hope so."

"That is very unlike you, and perhaps because you have been so lucky in your life, the moment has come when you have to pay, as everybody else does, for what you have received."

"You have forgotten your Bible," the Duke said mockingly. " 'An eye for an eye, and a tooth for a tooth.' That is justice!"

"If you read only a few more verses you will find that we should forgive our enemies."

"Perhaps I will do that, but only after they have been punished."

Lady Marguerite sighed.

"I have a feeling, Raven, that you are making yourself both judge and executioner, and that is a mistake."

"How can you be sure of that?" her brother asked. "And now I wish to see Anoushka."

He knew as he spoke that Lady Marguerite was regretting what she had told him, and perhaps regretting even the prayers she had expended in asking for a solution to her problem.

The Duke put out his hand to lay it on his sister's.

"Stop worrying, Marguerite," he said. "As you say, I have done many reprehensible things in my life, and I have gained a reputation which has undoubtedly shocked the elder members of the family. But I have never, as far as I can remember, done anything unsportsmanlike or behaved dishonourably to a woman who trusted me."

There was a note of sincerity in the Duke's voice, which made his sister look at him searchingly. Then she smiled.

"I know that is true, Raven, so I will trust you. But of course, whether you wish to marry Anoushka, whether she is the right person for you, is something you must decide for yourself."

"Exactly!" the Duke agreed.

His sister again rose to her feet.

"I will go now and find her. If she is not what you expect, or what you want, then you will have to look elsewhere."

The Duke did not reply, and only when his sister had left the room did he pour himself out another glass of wine and walk to the window.

He did not see the sunshine outside and the Nuns looking like flowers against the well-kept yew-hedges.

Instead he saw Cleodel's face in the moonlight as she smiled at Jimmy, then drew him from the balcony into her bedroom.

The Duke's fingers tightened on the stem of his glass until there was a faint sound and he realised he had cracked it.

It was then, as he prevented the wine from spilling to the floor, that he wished he could encircle Cleodel's white throat with his fingers and throttle her.

For the first time in his life he felt like murdering somebody, and he knew that what he wanted was undoubtedly an
eye for an eye and compensation for the murder of his
ideals.

That was what Cleodel had killed, the ideals that with her
youth and beauty she had resuscitated within him after he
had lost them in his philandering and raffish life.

Because she had stood for everything he ideally desired
in a woman, he had set her in a shrine in his heart that
before had always been empty.

Now she had despoiled and defiled it, and he hated her
with a violence that surpassed every emotion he had ever
felt before.

Yesterday in the train carrying him towards Paris he had
imagined the satisfaction he would have felt if he had followed his first impulse and climbed up onto the balcony to
enter Cleodel's bedroom.

He would have struck Jimmy and frightened Cleodel
until they had pleaded with him on their knees for mercy.

Then he realised that that would have been a very primi-
tive form of revenge which perhaps would have lowered
him to their level.

What he was planning now was far more subtle, far more
intelligent, and far more hurtful. Already he was quite
certain that Cleodel would be wondering frantically what
had happened and why he had not communicated with her.

Then this morning her father would have opened the
pages of *The Times* or *The Morning Post* and seen the announcement that the marriage had been postponed.

His consternation would be farcical, the Duke thought,
and he wished that he could only watch it.

He imagined the questions, the suppositions, the explanations the Earl and Cleodel would try to find. Then a letter
would be sent to Ravenstock House, and the Earl would
follow it and demand to see him and to be given an explanation.

The Duke was certain that Mr. Matthews would carry out his instructions to the letter.

Then there would be nothing the Sedgewicks could do but wait, and try to find answers to all the questions they wanted to ask while the wedding-presents continued to pour in.

The Duke gave a sharp laugh, and it was not a pleasant sound.

Yes, the revenge he had planned was far cleverer than anything that could be gained by physical violence, and when he took the next step in his plan, then there would really be consternation and speculation which would sweep through Mayfair like a tornado.

Cleodel, who would be at the centre of it, would eventually guess the reason for her fiancé's disappearance.

The smile on the Duke's lips deepened.

He heard the door open behind him and turned round.

Because he had been looking out into the sunlight, for the moment it was difficult for him to see at all clearly, but he heard his sister's voice say:

"Here is Anoushka!"

Chapter Three

LADY Marguerite moved towards her brother and as she reached him with the girl beside her she said:

"Let me, Anoushka, present my brother the Duke of Ravenstock."

Anoushka curtseyed. With the sun on her face, the Duke could now see her clearly, and she was not the least what he had expected.

Because he had been so bemused by Cleodel he had supposed that any very young girl he decided to marry would look in some way a replica of her — a young face, fair hair, blue eyes, and an expression that had seemed to him completely innocent.

But Anoushka was completely different.

She was slender, taller than average, and her face framed by the transparent veil of a Novice was so unexpected that he could not remember ever having seen a woman who looked in the least like her.

She was lovely in a very different way, and although he knew she was young she did not look it.

Instead, she had a kind of ageless beauty that he thought might be found on a Greek statue or perhaps engraved on the tombs in Egypt.

Her face was dominated by her large eyes, which seemed somehow mysterious and not what he would have imagined those of a young girl to be.

As he went on looking at her he realised that her nose was straight and classical and her lips might have been chiselled by a sculptor in Ancient Rome.

But what he had not expected, and what was so astonishing, was that she seemed to vibrate as a personality in a way that he had known before only when he had met people of great distinction in their own particular field.

He had been aware that a force and power radiated out from them in a manner that was impossible to put into words and yet was indisputably there.

At his first glance at Anoushka he could understand his sister finding her a problem and feeling that she should not and could not be confined within the walls of a Convent.

The Duke had the strange and fanciful idea that she was like an exotic bird imprisoned in a cage that was too small for her.

Then he told himself that he was being foolishly fanciful.

All he had asked for was a girl who was pure and un-touched, and this was what he was being offered.

Because he felt he must speak, he said to Anoushka:

"I understand from my sister that you have lived here for ten years?"

"That is true, *Monseigneur.*"

He noticed that she gave him the title reserved for the Princes of the Church, and he knew it was a compliment, although whether it was paid to himself or simply to his sister's brother he was not sure.

"And you have been happy here?"

"Very happy, *Monseigneur.*"

"Perhaps you found it strange after the life you led previously."

Anoushka did not reply, and he realised that she was not hesitating or choosing her words but was deliberately re-maining silent.

The Duke looked at his sister and Lady Marguerite said:

"Anoushka told me when she first came here that she had been instructed never to speak of where she came from, and she has obeyed those instructions to the letter."

The Duke wanted to ask why she should be so mysterious, and he thought that was the right word to describe her anyway. She was mysterious: an enigma that was intriguing although it might prove to be extremely irritating.

After a moment he said:

"I wonder, Marguerite, if it would be possible for me to talk to Anoushka alone? I think you would want to explain to her why I am here, but it is something I would prefer to do myself."

His request was obviously unexpected, and Lady Marguerite looked at him appealingly before she said in a low voice:

"Do you think that is — wise so — soon?"

"I see no point in waiting, and I have not the time to do so."

His sister's eyes searched his face.

He knew she was worried, almost distressed. At the same time, because he was the head of the family and, despite everything, she respected him, she was finding it hard to refuse.

"You can trust me," the Duke said with a smile, "not to do anything to upset Anoushka — or you."

Lady Marguerite drew in her breath. Then she said:"It is, as you well know, very unconventional, but I will leave you for ten minutes."

She walked towards the door, but before the Duke could move, Anoushka opened it and dropped a curtsey as her Mother Superior walked through it.

Then she shut the door quietly and turned round to look at the Duke.

Her eyes, which he now realised were so dark as to be almost purple, were watching his face.

He had the feeling that she was not looking at him as a handsome man, and this surprised him because she could not have seen many of them, and certainly none like himself.

It was as if she was looking far deeper than the surface, almost as if she searched for his soul.

Then the Duke said:

"Shall we sit down?"

She walked towards him with a grace that reminded him of Eastern women whom he had seen balancing water-vessels on their heads and moving like Queens.

With his hand he indicated the sofa, and when Anoushka sat on the edge of it, her back very straight, her eyes looking directly at him, he took an arm-chair facing her.

He noticed that she had the same stillness and serenity that he had always admired in his sister, and after a moment he said:

"My sister has told me your strange story, and also that she has decided that as you are now eighteen you should leave the Convent and see something of the world outside."

"I would like that."

"You do not wish to take your vows and become a Nun?"

"It is something I have considered, but it is difficult to make a judgement until I have seen the outside world, of which, living here, I know very little."

"That is understandable," the Duke said, "and because my sister has been worrying and praying over what would be best for you, I have what I think is an answer to her prayers and your problem."

He waited for Anoushka to ask him what this was, but she remained perfectly still, her eyes still looking at him speculatively as if, he thought, she weighed up everything he was saying.

Because he wished to surprise and perhaps startle her, he said abruptly:

"What I have to suggest is that you should marry me!"

Now there was undoubtedly an incredulous expression in her strange eyes, and it was only after a long silence that she said;

"Are you asking me, *Monseigneur,* to be your wife?"

"I would hope I could make you happy," the Duke replied, "and in case you do not understand, your position as my Duchess will be one of the most important in England."

"And you think I am suitable for such a position?"

"You will naturally have a lot to learn," the Duke replied, "but I will be with you to teach you and protect you from making mistakes."

As he spoke, he thought he was making it sound a proposition that was too businesslike, too cut-and-dried to appeal to a young girl.

But he felt that Anoushka would rather hear the truth frankly and honestly than have it dolled up in pretty phrases, although he had no idea why he should have thought that.

As he waited for her answer, he thought cynically that most women would go into raptures if he had even hinted at making them his wife.

"I have never thought of being married," Anoushka said in a low voice.

"If you are not anxious to become a Nun," the Duke said, "then surely marriage is the obvious alternative once you have left these Convent walls."

"It is a subject that has not appeared on the curriculum in my studies."

"Well, I hope you will now consider it," the Duke said. "I wish to marry immediately, for reasons I will not explain, and as we are in Paris I can easily provide you with a fashionable trousseau which any young woman would find exciting after wearing the robes you have on now."

As he spoke, he thought that this was an inducement no woman of his acquaintance could possibly resist.

Paris was the El Dorado of fashion, and the gowns of Frederick Worth which the Duke had bought for many of his mistresses meant as much to them as the jewels with which he encircled their necks or clasped in their ears.

But there was not the excitement that he looked for in Anoushka's eyes.

"You said," she remarked in her soft clear voice, "that

you will teach me how to be your wife. But suppose I fail and you are disappointed?"

The Duke realised she was thinking of him as one of the teachers who his sister had told him had been specially engaged for her studies because the money had been provided to pay for them.

"I have been told," the Duke replied, "how exceptionally intelligent you are. Therefore, I cannot imagine that you will find it hard to learn what you will find both interesting and enjoyable, and I assure you I am very experienced in the subjects we shall study together."

He smiled as he spoke because it seemed an almost ridiculous way to describe the union between a man and a woman.

Then as he did so he knew that to Anoushka what he was saying was serious and something she must contemplate with her brain.

It struck him then that because of her upbringing, her feelings had been subordinated entirely to her intellect, and he found himself wondering how long it would take before she would respond to him not as a teacher but as a man.

Anoushka was obviously turning over in her mind what had been said, and now she asked:

"Have I really a choice in what I do, or has the Reverend Mother decided I must leave the Convent with you, whether I wish it or not?"

The Duke was startled.

"I am sure that my sister would not force you to do anything you would not wish to do," he answered. "At the same time, may I say that what I am offering you is something which most women would be very eager to accept."

"I have a feeling that any other woman you would ask to be your wife, *Monseigneur,* would not be as ignorant or as inexperienced as I am. It would therefore be easier for them to adjust themselves to your requirements."

"I have already told you that I will prevent you from

making mistakes," the Duke said, "and as we shall not return to England for some time after we are married, we will
have a chance to get to know each other, which should make
things simpler than they would otherwise be."

Again there was silence. Then at length Anoushka said:

"May I have a little time, *Monseigneur,* to think this over?"

"Certainly," the Duke replied, "but I think you really
mean that you intend to pray about it."

Anoushka have him a faint smile.

"Here in the convent they are one and the same thing,
and it is easier to think in the Chapel."

The Duke rose to his feet.

"Very well then. I suggest that you go to the Chapel and I
will wait here until you are ready to give me your answer."

As he spoke, he felt that he was putting pressure on her.
But he knew she was suitable for his requirements and he
wished to get on quickly with his revenge on Cleodel.

"I will try not to be any longer than is necessary,"
Anoushka said in the same soft, quiet voice in which she had
spoken before.

She looked at him straight between the eyes as she spoke,
then curtseyed and moved towards the door.

The Duke did not open it for her, he only stood watching
her leave, thinking he had never before had such a strange
conversation with a woman.

Then he walked to the open window almost as if he
needed air.

Once again he looked grim as he planned his next move,
and it was one which Cleodel would find extremely unpleasant.

It was not more than five minutes before Lady Marguerite came back.

"I met Anoushka going to the Chapel," she said. "She told
me she was considering the suggestion you made to her and
she wishes to think about it."

The Duke gave his sister a rather wry smile.

"It is certainly unusual for any woman to wish to pray over any proposition I have made to her!"

"Anoushka is different, as I have already told you," Lady Marguerite said, "and I too have been thinking."

"And of course praying!" the Duke said almost mockingly.

His sister ignored the interruption and went on:

"If Anoushka decides to marry you, though there is always the possibility that she may refuse ... "

"Really, Marguerite," the Duke interposed, "are you seriously suggesting that a girl of eighteen would refuse to be the Duchess of Ravenstock?"

"You and I know what it means and entails," Lady Marguerite replied, "but to Anoushka it is just a name. Do remember, Raven, that she knows nothing of the world except what she has read in books, and those which come to the Convent are very carefully chosen, I can assure you."

The Duke did not reply and she went on:

"To Anoushka it would be like coming from another planet where they had never heard of the ordinary, everyday things that make up your life — racing, cards, Balls, dinner-parties, the Theatre!"

She paused, then went on:

"You and I know what those mean, and when I speak of them they conjure up for us memories of what we have seen and done. But to Anoushka they are just words of one, two, or three syllables!"

Lady Marguerite paused to see if her brother was following her, then finished:

"She cannot, however imaginative she may be, have any idea what such activities are really like, or the people who take part in them."

The Duke did not reply, and after a moment his sister said:

"Now that I have had more time to think about it, the whole idea seems absurd and quite impracticable! Go away,

Raven, and find some young woman who at least has been brought up in the same way as we were."

Her voice softened as she went on:

"I know something has upset and hurt you, but I do not feel that by marrying Anoushka you will feel any happier or give her the happiness she deserves."

"I intend to marry her," the Duke said.

There was an inflexible determination in the way he spoke, which told his sister that he was about to be difficult.

"I should not have mentioned her in the first place," she said as if she spoke to herself. "If she leaves here, I want her to find happiness."

"Which you are quite convinced I cannot give her."

"Let me put it another way," his sister replied. "I want her to find love, the love I knew with Arthur, the love that is so glorious and wonderful when a man and woman find it together that it is a gift from God."

The Duke moved restlessly across the room.

"And suppose she does not find this idealised love which happens, as you are aware, to very few people? Will you not feel you have deprived her of a position which most women would give their eyes to attain?"

"I understand what you are saying," Lady Marguerite replied, "of course I do. At the same time, Raven, I am frightened. For the first time in many years I feel indecisive and I do not know what is right or wrong. You are undermining my confidence in myself."

"Listen to me, Marguerite," the Duke said, "I came to you for help and you have given me what I asked for."

Lady Marguerite's eyes met her brother's defiantly, then as if she felt she could not go on fighting him she suddenly capitulated.

"Very well, Raven," she said, "I will allow you to marry Anoushka, as long as she agrees to do so, on one condition."

"What is that?"

"Because you are what you are—a very experienced,

sophisticated man with a reputation," Lady Marguerite
said, "I want you to give me your word of honour, which I
know you will not break, that while you marry Anoushka in
name, she remains as she is for three months — in your own
words, pure and untouched — before you actually make her
your wife."

The Duke looked at his sister reflectively.

"Do you think that is wise? I have always thought that any
marriage should be normal if it is to have a chance of being
successful."

"The marriage you are contemplating is not normal from
the very beginning," Lady Marguerite replied. "It is not
normal for you to come here demanding a girl who has
been brought up as a Novice."

Her voice sharpened as she went on:

"It is not normal for people in our position to marry out
of our class or, if you prefer it, our special environment, and
certainly it is not normal for you to find waiting for you, as if
by fate, somebody like Anoushka."

The Duke did not speak and Lady Marguerite said insistently:

"Promise me this, Raven, please promise me. You will set
my own mind at rest, and I believe it will eventually help you
and Anoushka to come to an understanding of each other."

There was a sob in her voice as she said:

"Because I love you I have always wanted your happiness
in a very different way from how you have found it up to
now."

"It is not wise to ask too much," the Duke replied lightly.

"Well, you and I at any rate could never tolerate second-
best!" Lady Marguerite flashed.

"That is true," the Duke replied.

As he spoke, he thought that that was what he had been
about to accept in Cleodel: second-best, skilfully disguised
with an intent to deceive.

Thinking how near he had been to making her his wife

and how later he would have realised he had been tricked and there would have been nothing he could do about it, he felt he should be grateful rather than angry.

"Do you need any money, Marguerite?" he asked unexpectedly. "I suppose I should express my gratitude to you in the usual manner."

Lady Marguerite shook her head.

"I am still a rich woman, Raven, which is why I am allowed to run the Convent very much my own way. But you can thank me by giving me your promise, which I have not yet received."

"Very well," the Duke conceded. "I promise!"

"And you may break it only if Anoushka asks you to do so."

"Thank you," the Duke said a trifle sarcastically.

He was thinking that he had never been with a woman who had not, with every word she spoke, every glance from her eyes, and every movement of her lips, invited his kisses and a great deal more.

He wondered how long it would be before Anoushka followed the example of all her predecessors, with of course the exception of Cleodel.

But she had Jimmy!

He had been making love to her when he was borrowing her father's horses. And perhaps every night when they were in London, Jimmy had sneaked up the ladder onto her balcony to share her bed.

Once again the Duke saw everything crimson before his eyes and felt his anger rising in his throat and almost choking him.

Then there was a knock at the door.

"Come in!" Lady Marguerite said.

It was Anoushka. She entered the room, closed the door behind her, and walked without hurry to where Lady Marguerite was standing.

She made a small curtsey, then stood straight and still, waiting for permission to speak.

Lady Marguerite looked at her."You have found the answer you were seeking, Anoushka?" she enquired.

"Yes, Reverend Mother."

"Will you tell me what it is?"

"I have decided I would like to accept the proposal the *Monseigneur* had made to me, but only, Reverend Mother, if you consider I am capable of fulfilling the position of his wife."

"I am sure you will do that very adequately, my dear."

Lady Marguerite looked towards her brother as she spoke, and the Duke, feeling as if he were taking part in a strange drama in which he was not quite certain if he was the hero or the villain, walked forward.

He took Anoushka's hand in his and lifted it perfunctorily to his lips.

"I am very honoured that you should accept me as your husband," he said quietly, "and I will do my uttermost to make you happy."

*

The Duke, having returned to his house in the Champs Élysées, sent for his French Secretary, *Monsieur* Jacques Tellier, who managed his possessions in France, and told him his exact requirements.

When he heard of the Duke's intention to be married the following morning, Jacques Tellier was obviously surprised, but at the same time he was too tactful to say so.

"My congratulations, *Monsieur le Duc,*" he said.

"I will go at once to *La Mairie* to make arrangements for the Civil Ceremony."

"Afterwards a quiet Service will take place at the Chapel attached to the Covent of the *Sacré-Coeur,*" the Duke said briefly.

As he spoke, he remembered that before he had left the convent he had said to his sister

'I presume Anoushka is a Catholic?"

"She came to our Services and was instructed by the Priests who are attached to the Convent ."

"What do you mean by that?" the Duke had asked, knowing the answer was not clear-cut.

'I have always had the feeling that before she came here, Anoushka had been brought up in the Russian Orthodox Church."

"Her name is certainly Russian, so her mother may have been Russian. But surely she would have told you so."

Lady Marguerite sighed.

"I do not really have time to explain it to you, but it was quite obvious that although she was only eight years of age, Anoushka had been told that she must never speak of her life before she was left on our doorstep, and because she is so different from other girls she never has done so."

"Not about anything?"

"Not about her religion, where she lived, who her parents were — nothing!"

"I cannot believe it !" the Duke said.

"It is certainly incredible. At first, because I thought she was suffering from the shock of separation from those she loved, I did not press her to tell me anything, but I thought it would gradually emerge."

"But it did not?"

"She had never dropped a hint or shown, either by her familiarity with anything or by her knowledge of anything different from what she was doing here, that she had known any other life."

"I find it very hard to believe," the Duke said.

"So did I," his sister agreed, "but, as I have told you, she is different from any other child I have ever met. Perhaps the Buddhists would account for it by saying she is a very old soul."

"So you think the religion in which she was brought up was Russian Orthodox?"

"I am only guessing," Lady Marguerite replied.

"It certainly seems very strange," the Duke said, "but I presume she will not object to being married as a Catholic to a Protestant?"

"I will ask her, but I feel she will make no objections," Lady Marguerite replied. "In fact, she doubtless knows already that you are not of her faith, because they all know here that I changed my Church when I came to France."

She smiled before she added:

"As you will understand, the younger Novices here are always very interested in asking me what my life was like when I was their age."

"And you tell them?" the Duke enquired.

"I tell them what I think is good for them to know," Lady Marguerite replied, and he laughed.

When the Duke had left the Convent he sent a groom to one of the most exclusive dressmakers in Paris.

It was no use asking *Monsieur* Worth for a gown, because he designed individually for each of his clients.

That, the Duke decided, would come later, but he wished Anoushka when she left the Convent to set aside all the trappings of a Novice and become at least superficially a wordly young woman dressed traditionally as a bride.

"It would be the start of her new life," he thought, "and as I intend it to continue."

It was not compulsory at a Civil Marriage for the bride to be present in front of the Mayor. Therefore, the Duke had attended to all the formalities and his Secretary had stood proxy for Anoushka,

When the documents had been prepared and stamped, the Mayor had taken him warmly by the hand and wished him a long life and many children.

The Duke had bowed his gratitude and wondered what the Frenchman would think if he knew that he had sworn that for three months his bride would remain untouched and as pure as when she had left the Convent.

When he went to bed the night before, he told himself that in a way it was a good idea.

He had no wish to make love to anybody at the moment, and he thought that even to touch Anoushka's lips would make him remember Cleodel and the passion she had aroused in him.

"How can I forget her?" he asked himself, and felt she would haunt him for the rest of his life.

When he came down to breakfast he sent for *Monsieur* Tellier and instructed him that a notice should be sent to the French newspapers and then telegraphed to the newspapers in London.

This was the moment he was waiting for and was the rapier-point of his revenge.

The notice had been worded very carefully:

His Grace the Duke of Ravenstock was married quietly in Paris yesterday. The Duke and Duchess, after a few days in the French Capital, will proceed on their honeymoon to Nice in the South of France.

The Duke had written it down in his own hand, then read the announcement and reread it to be quite certain that it was exactly what he required.

He only wished he could witness the consternation which such an announcement would produce when it was published in the English newspapers.

At first, he thought, his friends would find it so incredible that they would not believe it.

Then it would be realised that there was something strange about it; coming so shortly after the previous announcement that his wedding to Cleodel had been postponed.

It would not take long to discover that the bride was not the Earl of Sedgewick's daughter.

It was then that the gossip and speculation would sweep through Mayfair like a whirlwind.

"What can have happened?"

"Who can she be?"

"Why had the Sedgewicks no explanation?"

"How could the Duke, unpredictable though he is, have treated Lady Cleodel in such a way?"

Not even his closest friends like Harry would know the real answer, and perhaps only Jimmy would have a suspicion of the reason for his disappearance from London and his speedy marriage to somebody else.

He was sure that the women who had been jealous of Cleodel for succeeding where they had failed, and who had disliked her because she was young as well as lovely, would then gradually begin to guess what had happened.

Why should he run away, which was very unlike him, unless he had a good reason for doing so? The answer could lie only with the woman he had left behind.

It was a revenge even crueler and more hurtful because there would be nothing Cleodel could say, nothing she could do.

It had all happened too quickly for her to pretend that it was she who had changed her mind at the last moment or even that the Duke and she had quarrelled.

At first she and her parents would be too bewildered to find any plausible excuse for the sudden disruption of all their plans, and the Duke was sure that the only possible action they could take would be to leave London and retire to the country.

This would mean that once again Cleodel would have to forego the Balls at which she had shone so brilliantly.

She would not be able to attend the Assemblies and the Receptions that were such an intrinsic part of the Season, nor would she appear in the Royal Enclosure at Ascot.

Of course, she would have Jimmy.

But the Duke guessed cynically that Jimmy would be conspicuous by his absence and would make no effort to comfort the girl whom he had instructed so skilfully.

It was a revenge, the Duke congratulated himself, that few men would have had the intelligence to think out and few the audacity to carry through.

To make certain that nothing went wrong, he also sent the Courier who had accompanied him to Paris back to England to make sure the newspapers had the announcement exactly as he had expressed it.

After two days at Ravenstock House, he was to return to give a comprehensive report on exactly what had occurred.

"If any of Your Grace's friends wish to visit you in Paris, what shall I say, Your Grace?" the Courier asked.

"Tell them I am on my honeymoon and have no need for company other than that of my wife," the Duke replied. "You are to answer no questions about her, however hard you may be pressed on the subject."

To make quite certain that the Courier knew nothing, the Duke had arranged for him to leave Paris before the actual wedding took place, and he wondered how the Earl would approach the man, veering, he was sure, between bribery and bullying in order to learn what he wanted to hear.

There was an expression on the Duke's face that his sister would have recognised as one of cruelty, as, looking resplendent in the evening-dress in which every Frenchman was married, he was driven by his coachman down the Champs Élysées.

Because he was determined to start his marriage with Anoushka on what he thought was the "right foot," he was wearing the Order of the Garter across his right shoulder.

The Garter also glittered below his knee, and thought as he looked at himself in the mirror that it was a pity that Cleodel could not see him and be aware of what she had missed.

He realised now that under her soft, hesitating little act was an ambitious social-climber who was determined to get to the top of that prickly tree which so many had attempted to scale and failed.

But she had very nearly succeeded.

This was what infuriated the Duke more than anything else: the knowledge that he, who had always prided himself on his brains, his intuition, and his almost uncanny perception where pretence, hypocrisy, and insincerity were concerned, should have been caught by one of the oldest tricks in the world.

There was never a man born who did not feel protective and at the same time chivalrous towards a very young and innocent girl; there was never a man who did not like to think of himself as a Knight in shining armour, prepared to fight and kill the dragon that threatened the pure maiden.

The Duke could deride himself for being so gullible, but Cleodel had in fact played her part very cleverly, and of course Jimmy had been a good teacher.

"Damn them! Damn them!" the Duke wanted to cry out as he thought of how they must have plotted and planned every move of the game in which he had been as green as any yokel up from the country.

However, now he knew that he had the last laugh, and his revenge would brand Cleodel as clearly as if, like the Puritans in America, he had burnt an "A" for "Adultress" on her white skin — so very white, so soft to his touch.

Then he could see her again, the light in her eyes, the radiant smile on her lips as she looked at Jimmy on the balcony, and he knew that his revenge had so far not helped him to forget.

Chapter Four

THE Duke waited in the magnificent Salon of his house for Anoushka to come down to dinner.

Once again he was wearing the elegant evening-clothes in which he had been married, but without his decorations and the Order of the Garter.

As he sipped a glass of champagne, he thought that he had certainly had an unusual wedding, and very unlike what he had always anticipated he would have.

The marriage he had planned with Cleodel would have been one of the events of the Season, with St. George's Church packed to overflowing with the elite of the country, and leading the distinguished guests present would have been the Prince and Princess of Wales.

The Queen would have sent a representative, and there would have been members of many European Royal families present to make it such a distinguished occasion that it would have been talked about long after it had taken place.

The Reception at Ravenstock House would have filled the Ball-Room to capacity, and if some of the guests preferred to walk in the garden, his gardeners had been working over the last month to make it a picture of perfection.

Instead, the only witnesses of his marriage to Anoushka had been his sister, Lady Marguerite, and an elderly Nun who played the organ with what the Duke recognised as outstanding skill.

He had expected that the other members of the Convent would be present, but then he had realised that it might have distracted them from their quiet life and perhaps put unsuitable ideas into the Novices' heads.

Therefore, on arrival at the Convent, the Nun who had opened the door had escorted him straight up to the Chapel where his sister was waiting for him.

"I thought you should know, Raven, that the Bishop of Paris, under whose aegis we are as a Convent, has come especially to marry you," she had said. "He will be supported by our usual Priest and two Servers. Otherwise there will be nobody in the Chapel but ourselves."

The Duke had smiled.

"A quiet marriage, Marguerite," he had said, "and the way I would wish it to be."

"If you will go in," his sister had replied, "I will bring Anoushka."

The Duke had walked into the small Chapel which he felt was redolent with the faith of those who worshipped there.

The Bishop and the other Priest were wearing spectacularly ornate white robes which he guessed had been embroidered in the Convent, and the altar was massed with flowers.

The organ played softly, and after he had waited a few minutes his sister came up the aisle with Anoushka walking beside her.

The Duke turned to watch their progress and realised that Anoushka, wearing the wedding-gown he had sent her, for the first time since she was eight was not dressed in the robes of a Novice.

The gown he had sent was softly draped at the front and swept to the back with frill upon frill of pleated gauze to make both a bustle and a train.

He had also ordered a fine lace veil which covered her face, and her head was encircled by a small wreath of orange-blossoms.

She did not carry the bouquet he had sent her, but instead

she held in her hand a Prayer-Book with a mother-of-pearl cover, which the Duke suspected belonged to his sister.

He noted that Anoushka walked proudly with her head up, and her eyes were not on the ground as was usual when a bride approached the altar and her bridegroom.

Instead, through her veil he could see her looking at him and he wondered what she was thinking.

The Service began, and as it was a marriage of mixed religions it was very short.

The Bishop blessed them with a sincerity that made the Duke feel somewhat ashamed.

His marriage was taking place primarily — in fact entirely — as an act of revenge, and he could not help remembering his sister's words that she wanted Anoushka to find the love that she herself had found with Arthur Lansdown before he had died.

"I will be kind to her and give her everything she wants," the Duke vowed pensively to himself, and knew at the same time that what he was doing was intrinsically wrong.

When the marriage was over and the Duke walked out of the Chapel with Anoushka on his arm, he knew his sister expected them to leave immediately.

"The carriage is waiting, Raven," she said, "and I can only give you my good wishes and pray ceaselessly that you will both be very happy."

She looked at the Duke as she spoke, and he knew exactly what she was saying to him.

He kissed first her cheek, then her hand.

"Thank you, Marguerite," he said.

He helped Anoushka into the closed carriage that was waiting, and as they drove away he turned sideways to look at his bride, thinking that he had had no opportunity to do so until now.

Her veil was thrown back over her head so that he could see her hair for the first time.

He had thought it was dark, but now he saw that it was a strange, indeterminate colour to which he could not put a name.

Perhaps, he thought, it was the result of her parents having different nationalities, It seemed almost to have silver streaks against a colour that was neither dark nor fair, and made him think of the ashes of a burnt-out fire.

Once again he realised how different her beauty was from that of any other girl he had known.

Then as he went onlooking at her, her eyes met his and she asked anxiously:

"Do . . . do I look . . . all right? I feel very . . . strange, and when I first saw this gown it made me . . . laugh."

"Laugh?" the Duke questioned.

She smiled, which he had never seen her do before, and her face seemed suddenly transformed as if by sunshine.

"I thought it seemed very amusing that a gown should have so much decoration at the back and so little at the front," she explained.

"That is the vogue set by Mr. Worth, who is the King of Fashion," the Duke replied.

He realised that Anoushka was looking at him to see if he was serious.

"Are you saying that a man made this gown?"

"He designed it," the Duke corrected, "but he has over a thousand people working for him."

Anoushka laughed, and he thought it was a very pretty sound, clear and spontaneous, and quite different from the rather affected laughter of other women he knew.

"I cannot imagine a man designing gowns for women," she said, "I thought sewing was an entirely feminine occupation."

When the Duke laughed, she said:

"I was thinking last night what a lot of things I have to

learn, but if they are all going to be like my gowns, then I shall find them very funny."

That was true, the Duke thought now, and if Anoushka had been surprised at what she saw and heard, he was astonished at her reactions to the new world, which, as his sister had said, was to her like stepping onto another planet.

When they had first talked together she had been dressed as a Novice and she had been very serious as she considered whether she should or should not marry him.

He had therefore anticipated that he would find her seriously weighing up everything she discovered and approaching it in the same manner as that of a pupil attending a lesson with a teacher.

Yet, so many things seemed to amuse her that the Duke found himself laughing too, and the afternoon passed very differently from what he had expected.

He found that when she was animated, especially when she was laughing, her face had a new beauty that rather intrigued him, and she had a sparkle in her eyes which for the moment at any rate swept away the mystery in them.

Above all, he liked the sound of her laughter.

It struck him halfway through the afternoon that Cleodel had seldom laughed, but when she did so it was a hesitating little sound as if she forced it to her lips, in the same way as she had made her voice sound shy, young, and a little nervous.

As the Duke thought of her, there was a frown between his eyes and his lips tightened.

Anoushka, who had been inspecting the paintings in his house, turned from one of them which they had been discussing to ask him a question, then the words died on her lips.

"What have I . . . said which is . . . wrong?" she asked.

"I did not hear what you asked me," the Duke admitted.

"B-but you are . . . angry."

"Not with you," he replied quickly. "It was just something I thought of."

He tried to smooth away the frown and force a smile to his lips, but he realised that Anoushka was looking at him in the same way as she had done at the Convent when he had felt she was looking beneath the surface and seeking his soul.

Because he could not help being curious, he asked:

"What are you thinking?"

She did not reply but turned her head away to look at the painting.

"I asked you a question, Anoushka,"

"I . . . I do not wish to . . . answer it," she replied,"because it might be . . . something you do not . . . wish to hear."

The Duke paused for a moment before he said:

"I think we should establish now, once and for all, that as we are married it would be a mistake for us not to be frank with each other. You have asked me to teach you, so I shall tell you honestly if you are doing or saying something wrong, and I shall not expect you to be offended."

"No, of course not," Anoushka said quickly.

"And the same applies to me," the Duke said. "I will not be offended or upset at anything you say to me, and let me beg of you to be frank and truthful. The one thing I will not tolerate is if you lie to me."

He spoke almost furiously as he remembered how Cleodel had lied to him.

"I will not lie," Anoushka said, "and the answer to your question is that what you were thinking was . . . ugly, and in some way it . . . spoilt you."

The Duke stared at her.

"What do you mean — spoilt me?" he enquired.

"You look so magnificent but it is not only how you look," Anoushka replied. "I think you are also noble, kind, and compassionate, which is why I agreed to . . . marry you."

She paused, and as the Duke could not find words in which to reply, she went on:

"Because just now you were . . . different from what you have appeared before, I . . . thought it was something you should control and forestall."

The Duke was speechless.

Anoushka had spoken to him in a quite impersonal manner, which he realised was the way he had been speaking to her.

There was nothing intimate about it, nothing of the soft allurement which might have been expected to pass between a man and a woman, even if they were not attracted to each other.

Instead it was an entirely logical, dispassionately thought-out appraisement, and he was intelligent enough to recognise it as such.

"I understand what you are saying," he said after a moment, "and thank you for being so honest with me."

"You are like your paintings," Anoushka said, "and I could not bear to think that any of them might be damaged."

Then, as if the subject was closed, she asked him questions about the very fine examples of pink Sèvres porcelain, which led the Duke to tell her the story of how *Madame* de Pompadour had started a China Factory.

She listened to him attentively. Then she said:

"I have read about *Madame* de Pompadour in one of the history-books, but when I asked my teacher about her she refused to answer, saying she was not a woman with whom I should concern myself. Why was that?"

The Duke thought this was a hurdle he would have to jump sooner or later, and he replied:

"She was the mistress of Louis XV."

"What does that mean?"

"You have no idea?"

"Not really," Anoushka replied. "In the history-books of France there seem to have been a lot of women who wielded great power though they were not aristocrats. How am I to understand if nobody will explain to me why they were so important?"

The Duke thought for a moment. Then he said:

"The Kings of France, like Kings everywhere, had their wives chosen for them for reasons of policy, so that the uniting of two Royal families might strengthen their throne or their country."He paused.

"But because he was also a man with ordinary desires, the King often chose a woman whom he found attractive to be his companion."

As the Duke spoke he watched Anoushka's face and knew by the expression in her eyes that she was trying to understand exactly what he was saying.

"Did the King love the woman who was his mistress?" she asked.

"Usually," the Duke replied, "and Louis XV not only loved *Madame* de Pompadour but was faithful to her, which was unusual."

"You mean that some Kings have had more than one mistress?"

"I see you will have to read about Charles II of England," the Duke said, "who had many mistresses, all of them very beautiful, one of the most important being a Frenchwoman. I have a portrait of Louise de Keroualle in my house in the country, which is one of the finest that was ever painted of her."

Anoushka did not speak for a few seconds. Then she asked:

"If Kings have mistresses, do ordinary men have them too?"

"Only when they can afford them."

"You mean . . . they are expensive? Why?"

"A mistress expects to be rewarded for her services . . ." the Duke began.

"What do those services entail?" Anoushka interrupted.

The Duke thought for a moment.

He felt it might be a mistake to pursue this conversation so soon after they were married. At the same time, it was inevitable sooner or later in the world in which Anoushka would live with him.

"A mistress reciprocates her protector's attention as best she can," he said, "and you will learn, Anoushka, that she expects to be paid, either with money or jewellery, for her kisses and any further show of affection a man requires of her."

Anoushka thought this over in silence until she said:

"It seems . . . very strange. I always thought that love would be given and was not something for which one would expect . . . payment of any sort."

The Duke appreciated the quickness of her mind, but he said:

"I suggest we leave this subject. It is certainly not something we should be discussing on our wedding-day."

Anoushka looked at him.

"I think because you say that it means that you have had mistresses you would not wish me to know about."

"If I have, it is not something I should be discussing with my wife," the Duke retorted.

He spoke sharply, then realised it was a mistake.

"I am . . . sorry if that was . . . wrong of me," Anoushka said humbly, "but you . . . did say we were to be . . . frank with each other."

The Duke felt as if he had walked into a maze and for the moment had lost his way.

"I meant what I said," he replied. "It is just that today, of all days, I want you to learn about things that are beautiful, like my paintings and a great many other things in this house."

"I understand," Anoushka said, "and everything you tell me is of interest to me."

The Duke knew this was true, and a little later, when he thought his explanations to Anoushka's questions had been very skilful, he said:

"Tomorrow I intend to take you to meet *Monsieur* Worth and get him to design some special gowns for you that will express your personality and your individuality. Only he can do that, which is the reason why he is hailed as a genius."

He thought Anoushka looked pleased, and he went on:

"Tonight when you go upstairs to dress for dinner you will find several gowns waiting for you that I have ordered to tide you over until Worth's creations are ready, and I hope that the bonnets and the other accessories that go with them will please you."

"I hope somebody will show me how to put them on."

"An experienced lady's-maid will do that," the Duke replied, "and as a *Coiffeur,* the most famous in Paris, is coming to style your hair, I think you will soon begin to feel you are a very different person from the one you have been in the past."

"A *Coiffeur?*" Anoushka questioned. "That means a hair-dresser."

The Duke smiled.

"Another man!" he said. "Henri is the most famous *Coiffeur* in Paris. It is not only difficult to obtain his services, but he charges an astronomical sum to attend you."

"I can see it is very expensive to be a Lady of Fashion," Anoushka said. "I am only hoping you will think I am worth it."

Because her eyes were so expressive, the Duke knew he could read her thoughts: she was thinking that in accepting so much from him it was almost as if she were his mistress.

He wondered what she would say if he explained exactly what was expected of a mistress and also a wife.

Then he remembered his promise to his sister, and

thought that as they had three months of chastity imposed upon them, it would be a mistake to talk too soon of things which might make his promise hard to keep.

*

The door of the Salon opened and Anoushka came in.

She was wearing another exquisitely beautiful gown which became her even though it did not have the special, unique touch that only Worth could impart.

It was made of very pale pink tulle with a bustle billowing out behind it and with tulle framing her shoulders, which the Duke realised for the first time were pearly white.

She looked so lovely as she advanced towards him that he felt as if he should applaud.

Henri had certainly created a masterpiece with her hair. It was coiled round her head in the way that the Princess of Wales had made fashionable in England, and it accentuated the Grecian look that the Duke had noticed the first time he had seen her.

At the same time, he thought that while she had none of Cleodel's pink-and-white, little-girl prettiness, she indeed looked young, pure, and untouched in a way that was more spiritual than physical.

She came towards him and as she reached him she laughed.

"You are right, *Monseigneur*," she said. "I feel very unlike myself. In fact when I looked in the mirror I saw a stranger staring at me. But there is one thing that worries me."

Her laughter died away and now she looked at him a little nervously.

"What is it?" the Duke asked.

"Is it really correct and not immodest to . . . wear so little on my . . . chest and arms?"

The Duke noted that she did not blush because he was a man looking at her, but her eyes were as uncertain as her voice.

"You will find," he replied, "that you would look very strange indeed if your evening-gowns were not exactly like the one you are wearing now, with perhaps an even lower décolletage."

"What is the idea?" Anoushka asked. "It is colder at night than it is in the day, and it seems more sensible to be covered up, especially in the winter."

"But not so attractive," the Duke said. "When you see a Ball-Room filled with women dressed as you are now, they look like beautiful swans gliding round the room, and the men who partner them appreciate the whiteness of their skin."

He did not wait for Anoushka's reply but went on:

"As I appreciate yours. I have a present for you."

He picked up a green leather box from the table beside him and held it out to her.

"This is . . . for me?" she asked.

"A wedding-present," the Duke replied. "And because we have been married in such haste, we have, I am glad to say, no letters of thanks to write, and no rose-bowls, entrée dishes, or candelabra we do not want."

"Is that what people generally send when one is married?"

"Dozens of them," the Duke answered, thinking of the presents laid out in the Ball-Room at Ravenstock House.

"Do the bridegroom and the bride give each other presents?" Anoushka enquired. "I have nothing for you."

"You can buy me a present later if you wish to do so," the Duke replied.

"But . . . I have no money."

"My sister did not explain to you that you are in fact a very rich young woman?"

"Is . . . that . . . true? Then . . . Pap . . . ."

The Duke realised she had been about to say the word "Papa," then had stopped herself.

"I would like you to finish that sentence, Anoushka."

She shook her head, and he said:

"I think you were going to speak of your father."

Anoushka was looking down at the green box he had put into her hands.

She opened the lid to see arranged on black velvet a diamond necklace, bracelet, ear-rings, and a ring.

They flashed and glittered as she stared at them, and the Duke realised that she had no intention of answering his question.

"I hope these will give you pleasure," he said. "They will belong to you personally, although there are also a great number of very fine jewels which are heirlooms worn by every Duchess of Ravenstock."

"They are ... very beautiful," Anoushka said, "and I never thought I should own anything like this, although I have seen such jewels in pictures and drawings."

"These are yours," the Duke said, "and I will show you how to put them on."

As he spoke, he took the necklace from the box and put it round her neck, fastening it skilfully at the back.

He found himself thinking how many necklaces he had given in the past to women who had always been eager for jewels, but this was certainly the first time he had ever given them to a woman who had never owned any before.

Having fastened the necklace, he took the ear-rings and fixed them to the small lobes of her ears.

He had ordered them to be made specially for ears that had not been pierced, and he thought that as hers were so small she might find the ear-rings heavy and difficult to keep on.

Only as he fixed the second one did he realise that Anoushka could see her reflection in the mirror over the mantelpiece and was watching what he was doing.

Then she gave one of her spontaneous little laughs and said:

"I would feel like a Queen if I had a crown."

"Are you in an obscure way asking for a tiara?" the Duke enquired.

She looked at him to see if he was serious before she answered:

"I would never ask for anything when you have been so generous to me already, and I know what a tiara is. Will I have to wear one now that I am your wife and we go to parties?"

"Invariably," the Duke replied. "In London every woman wears a tiara at the big Balls and Receptions, and especially when they dine at Marlborough House with the Prince and Princess of Wales."

For a moment he thought Anoushka looked nervous. Then she said, as if she was consoling or comforting herself:

"I suppose really it is only a jewelled bonnet."

The Duke laughed.

"A very good description, but there is no need to be nervous. I will tell you what you must wear and when you should wear it."

"That is what I would like you to do," Anoushka said, "but as you have already chosen my new gowns, I wonder how you know so much about how a woman should look, when I am sure most women have no idea what a man should wear?"

She spoke as if she was thinking out loud. Then she said quickly:

"Do not answer that question. I am sure I am talking nonsense. It only seems strange to me, since, having always been with women who know nothing about men, it never struck me that men would know about us."

"Not about Nuns," the Duke agreed, "but about ordinary women with whom I and most other men like to spend a lot of time."

"Why?" Anoushka enquired.

"Because I find women extremely attractive, I like to look at them, admire them, and . . ."

The Duke hesitated. Then he took the plunge:

". . . sometimes to make love to them."

"Even when you are not married?"

The Duke nodded.

"Then the ladies to whom you make love are your mistresses?" Anoushka said.

"Not always," the Duke replied. "As I said this afternoon, it is too soon to explain a somewhat complicated subject in detail."

As he spoke, he was thinking that it would be very difficult for him to put into words the difference between a mistress who was a Courtesan, or what the Bible termed a "harlot," and a Lady with whom one had an *affaire de coeur*.

However, he was saved from answering any more of Anoushka's questions because as he clasped the diamond bracelet round her wrist and put on her finger the ring which matched the whole suite, the Butler announced dinner.

After an excellent meal in the candlelit Dining-Room, the table decorated with white flowers, the Duke did not linger over his port but went with Anoushka to the Salon.

"As the night is so young," he said, "I thought it might amuse you to visit one of the places of amusement in Paris. There are quite a number of them, of which I suppose you are not aware, and tomorrow we might go to the Theatre."

Anoushka's eyes widened.

"Can we really do that?"

"There is nothing to stop us, unless you do not want to see a Play or listen to an Opera."

"But I would like to do both!"

"Then you will certainly have your wish," the Duke answered. "Tonight I will take you to a Restaurant where there is also dancing and we will have supper there."

"You realise I cannot dance?" Anoushka asked in a low voice.

"You shall have lessons as soon as I can arrange it," the

Duke said. "In the meantime I will teach you a few steps myself."

"That would be very exciting, but I wonder what the Mother Superior would say."

"You are not at the Convent now," the Duke replied, "and the only person to whom you are responsible for your behaviour is your husband."

"I feel rather embarrassed at being so ignorant of all the things you do and also the things you talk about," Anoushka said.

"There is no reason to feel like that," the Duke replied. "I have promised to teach you, and let me say I find it an intriguing task, especially as you react to most of the new things you encounter in a different way from what I expected."

"What did you expect?" Anoushka asked.

The Duke considered for a moment.

"A frightened young woman who would be prudish and disapproving of most of the things I have suggested."

Anoushka smiled.

"I do not wish to disapprove of anything," she said. "It is only that everything is so strange, but at the same time so funny."

"What is funny now?" the Duke enquired.

"I was thinking how funny the servants look dressed up in that elaborate livery and the food on silver plates which must be very valuable. It is funny too that you have so many houses belonging to you when you are a man alone, without a wife to entertain for you and with no children."

"That is something that can be remedied in the future," the Duke said in a quiet voice.

"You mean that we can have children?" Anoushka enquired.

"I sincerely hope so."

"I would like that," she said, "but how can we do it? They always talked at the Convent about our being the 'children of God,' but they never explained how, as we had ordinary parents, we came into the world."

"As this is a subject which we must find time to talk about, shall we postpone it for the moment?" the Duke asked. "The carriage is waiting now to take us to see the bright lights of Paris."

Anoushka smiled and he saw the excitement in her eyes.

A servant produced a fur-trimmed wrap which matched her gown, and the Duke allowed his red-lined cape to be placed over his shoulders, and took his tall hat, gloves, and ivory-headed cane from one of the footmen.

As the Duke joined Anoushka in the carriage, she asked:

"Why are you carrying a stick? We are not walking."

"It is the correct thing to carry in the evening," he replied.

"Like a lady carrying a fan?"

"Exactly!"

"I think it is a funny thing to do."

"I have never thought about it," the Duke admitted, "but I suppose it is, in a way, just as it is unnecessary really to carry gloves which are seldom put on."

"I am putting mine on. Is that correct?"

"Of course," he answered. "A lady should always wear gloves when she is not at home."

"Always?"

"It would be thought strange if her hands were bare."

"But we can have a bare chest?"

"It may seem somewhat incongruous," the Duke said, "but I do not set the fashions, which have evolved ever since Eve was particular about what shaped fig-leaf she should wear!"

Anoushka's laughter rang out.

"Do you really think there was fashion in the Garden of Eden? Whenever our Priests told us the story of how Adam and Eve were expelled after they had realised they were naked, they always seemed to hurry over how they clothed themselves when they were outside in the wilderness."

"I am sure they found it embarrassing to talk to young girls about nakedness," the Duke said.

"It cannot really be wrong if we are all born naked," Anoushka argued.

"I have not said it is wrong," the Duke replied, "but it would be cold if you went about without clothes, and certainly you would be very disillusioned when you realised that someone whom you admired very much in a gown such as you are wearing now had very ugly legs, or a thick waist."

Anoushka laughed again.

"We were never allowed to talk about our legs at the Convent and some of the girls had very fat ones. I am glad mine are thin."

The Duke wondered if he dared say that he was looking forward to seeing them, then decided that was too intimate.

He realised that Anoushka was talking to him quite naturally, as she might have talked to another girl, and he thought that when he had asked for a wife who was pure and untouched he might also have added the word "unawakened."

That was what Anoushka was, he thought, completely unawakened to the fact that a man could be an attractive being, and that her feeling for one could be something very different from what she felt towards a Priest, who was the only type of man she had seen up to now.

Unless of course she could remember the men she had encountered before she had been left at the Convent.

He thought over how she had nearly spoken of her father when he had told her she was rich, and he was sure that she was about to say that if she had money it meant that her father was dead.

As they drove on he told himself that sooner or later he would get her to talk about her past and discover exactly who she was.

It would be intriguing to try to find out where she came from, who were her parents, and what was her name.

If there was one thing the Duke enjoyed, it was being challenged either to prove himself in the field of sport or to use his brain in some unexpected manner.

Now he found himself determined, however difficult it might be, to unravel the tangled chain of events which had brought Anoushka to the Convent, to discover who had paid for her education there and finally had left her what to any woman was a considerable fortune.

Because of what she had so very nearly said, he felt sure now it must have been her father, but if so, why had he never been to see her?

Why had he hidden her in that mysterious way?

It would have been more understandable if it was her mother who, having produced a "love-child" had placed her in the Convent for safety, and then had somehow been able to provide such large sums of money for her.

"I must get to the bottom of this," the Duke told himself.

He felt a sudden enthusiasm for the task he had been set, and it swept away for the moment at any rate the haunting memory of Cleodel.

*

The place to which the Duke took Anoushka was one of the most respectable Restaurants in Paris, but after the dinner was over the tables in the centre of the room were cleared and a Band played popular dance-tunes.

The Duke had been given one of the alcoves that surrounded half the room where they were a little raised above the tables on the floor and therefore had a better view of the dancers.

Having dined so well at home, the Duke ordered only champagne and some spoonfuls of caviar, which he was sure Anoushka would never have eaten before.

When it came, he thought, she looked at it in surprise, and he explained:

"This is caviar. It comes from Russia and is one of the great specialties that gourmets enjoy."

"Caviar!" Anoushka said almost beneath her breath, and there was a lilt in the tone which the Duke did not miss.

"You have heard of it?" he asked.

"I thought I should never eat it again!" she replied.

The Duke did not reply. He only knew this was another clue and a very helpful one.

He had been sure, from what his sister had said, that Anoushka's mother must have been Russian.

He remembered that when he had visited St. Petersburg five years ago, the women he had met at the Winter Palace were all extremely beautiful and that many of them had the large, mysterious eyes that he thought might almost be replicas of Anoushka's.

At the same time, she did not look completely Russian, and he knew that was because her father was English.

It was the combination of the two that made her look so unusual.

He waited until she had finished her portion of caviar, eating it quickly with a fork and refusing the hot toast she was offered to go with it.

"Will you have some more?" he enquired.

Anoushka looked at him doubtfully.

"Would it be greedy if I said 'yes'?"

"I want you to enjoy yourself," the Duke said, "and I am glad you like caviar. It is something I like too, and I am quite sure it is a delicacy they did not provide you with at the Convent."

"I am sure, with the exception of the Reverend Mother, none of the Nuns had ever even heard of it."

"I am surprised that you liked it when you were a child," the Duke said, thinking he was being rather subtle. "I feel most children would think it greasy."

Anoushka did not reply.

She merely looked at the dancers and after a moment said:

"I think the Reverend Mother would be shocked by the sight of a gentleman putting his arms round a lady's waist."

"But the Reverend Mother is not here," the Duke said, "but I am. And I think, as we agreed to be frank with each other, that you are evading my questions."

She looked at him before she said:

"Please . . . you must not be angry . . . but . . . it is something I cannot . . . answer."

"Why not?"

"Because I have . . . given my word."

"To whom?"

"That is another question to which I cannot . . . reply".

"I can understand your keeping your words of honour to everybody except one particular person," the Duke said.

"Who. . . is that?"

"Your husband. You must realise that the Marriage Service today made us one person, and therefore our loyalty is not to anybody else but only to each other."

Anoushka was silent for a moment before she asked:

"Are you . . . sure that is . . . right?"

"It is how I interpret the marriage-ceremony, and I am sure if you ask your Father Confessor he will tell you the same thing."

Anoushka sighed.

"I think you must explain to me what is expected when one is married, since the Nuns and Novices never had husbands and are not allowed to talk about them."

"But now you are married," the Duke said, "and I am here to explain to you what a husband means, and also what a wife should and should not do."

Anoushka was looking not at him but at the dancers, and yet he was aware that she was listening to him.

Then the Duke thought again that it would be a mistake

to get involved in such a difficult conversation so soon after they were married.

And yet, because he was aware that, ignorant though she was, Anoushka had a quick and very intelligent brain, he told himself it was going to be difficult to keep to commonplace and banal subjects when there were such intriguing fundamental ones waiting for them, all of which he knew opened up new horizons which she did not even dream existed.

Then he realised that she was not only very lovely but unique.

He did not miss the glances she had received when they had come in and the way the men at the adjacent tables kept looking at her.

He knew she was supremely unaware of their admiration, intent only on looking at what was happining, with the eyes of a child.

"That is what she is in so many ways," the Duke thought to himself. "At the same time, she has a brain which when it is developed will make many men look foolish."

The dance-floor was now crowded, and as one couple who had obviously had too much to drink bumped into another couple, one of the woman slipped and fell down on the floor.

Anoushka gave a little gurgle of laughter.

"Has that happened because the floor is so slippery?" she asked.

"No, it is because those people have been drinking too much and are unsteady on their feet," the Duke replied.

"I have heard of drunkenness," Anoushka said, "but I did not know it made it difficult to walk or to dance."

"In most cases it means that people are rather noisy and laugh too much."

He saw the look of apprehension on Anoushka's face as

she pushed her glass of champagne to one side, as if she was afraid to drink any more.

"You need not worry that it will happen to you," he said. "I have told you I will look after you."

"Please do that," Anoushka said. "I would be horrified at myself if I behaved like the woman over there!"

The Duke watched the woman now giggling stupidly as two men tried to lift her to her feet.

Then as the other dancers passed they looked at her contemptuously, raising their eye-brows and shrugging their shoulders in a typically French fashion.

"I think it is . . . degrading," Anoushka said, "for a woman to . . . behave like that. I do not . . . like to see it. Please . . . can we . . . go?"

The Duke put a number of franc-notes on the table and rose to his feet.

"Of course," he said. "It was a mistake to bring you here in the first place."

They walked out of the Restaurant, the carriage was called, and when it arrived the Duke told his servants to open the hood.

As they drove off with the stars shining above them, Anoushka said in a nervous little voice:

"Perhaps it was . . . wrong of me to ask you to take me away . . . I am . . . sorry if I . . . spoilt your enjoyment."

"You did nothing of the sort," the Duke answered. "What you have just seen is something which I am sure rarely happens at that particular Restaurant. You were just unfortunate, and it is not the sort of behaviour you are likely to come in contact with elsewhere."

As he finished speaking he realised that Anoushka was not listening.

Instead, she was looking up at the stars with her head thrown back. The line of her long neck had an almost classical beauty as they passed the street-lights which revealed both her profile and the glitter of diamonds on her white skin.

She looked ethereal, and after a moment she said:

"The sky is so beautiful at night, and it seems strange that men and women do not look at the stars instead of dancing in a small stuffy room."

"They dance because they want to be close to each other," the Duke replied, "and the stars are far away."

Anoushka turned her head to look at him.

"Are you saying that the men and women we saw tonight dancing together want to be close to each other because they are . . . in love?"

"No, of course not," the Duke replied. "But most women who are unmarried are seeking a husband, and men like to dance with any woman they find attractive."

Anoushka thought this over. Then she said:

"I do not think I really want to dance, but if I did, it would be much more pleasant to dance alone."

Chapter Five

THE following day, the Duke thought, was filled with Anoushka's laughter.

There were so many things that amused her, to his surprise, since he had never thought of them as being in the slightest degree funny.

First, she had found the Champs Élysées as alluring as did the children who flocked there every morning.

Green and picturesque with the great private mansions scattered amongst the trees, it also provided numerous side-shows with Punch and Judy, roundabouts, miniature carriages drawn by goats, and stalls selling toys, gingerbread, and balloons.

As he watched Anoushka's eyes shining and listened to her exclamations of joy and the sound of her laughter, the Duke realised that this could not have been part of her childhood.

He longed to ask her questions, but he knew if he did so she would lapse into one of those repressive silences which he could not break.

Instead he drove her round Paris in an open Chaise to see the sights.

The half-finished Eiffel Tower made her laugh too.

"Who could have thought of such a monstrous monument?" she asked when he expalined that it was to be the centre-point of an Exhibition.

"I agree it is not particularly beautiful," the Duke replied, "but at the same time there will be a magnificent view from the top of it when it is finished."

When they drove beside the Seine, Anoushka did not

laugh, but she was fascinated by the animated scene on the great river, with its *bateaux-mouches* gaily decorated with pendants and streamers, and the *bateaux-lavoirs* for washer-women.

When they were driving along the wide boulevards, Anoushka was again laughing at the strange people sitting outside the *Cafés*, the Dandies, and the ladies of both the *Monde* and the *demi-monde* displaying the latest and most outrageous fashions.

She still found the bustle funny, although her own gown had one which was so skilfully made that on Anoushka it did not seem an exaggerated form of dress but added to her grace and the dignity with which she moved.

Finally the Duke took her to meet Frederick Worth in the Rue de la Paix.

He was used to women for whom he had bought clothes speaking of Worth almost as if he were a god.

They treated him with a reverence that made the Duke feel that they were quite prepared to kneel down and worship him if he would create for them the gowns they wanted. Therefore, he was not prepared for Anoushka's reaction.

Now as he looked through her eyes at the great man who came from Lincolnshire and who had slept under the counter as an apprentice, the Duke could understand the quiver at the corners of her mouth and the irrepressible twinkle that lit the purple of her pupils.

In his fur-trimmed velvet coat, with the beret he always wore on his greying hair, and speaking in his bombastic manner, Worth, when thought of as an ordinary man, was indeed funny.

Because he knew the Duke was very rich, the famous designer studied Anoushka closely, then appreciatively.

There was silence as he walked round her, regarding her from every angle before he said, and his voice was entirely sincere:

"It will be a pleasure and a privilege to dress somebody whose beauty is so different from that of my other customers."

Anoushka looked at the Duke to see if what Frederick Worth was saying pleased him.

"That is what I thought myself," the Duke said quietly, "and my wife needs an entire trousseau as quickly as you can provide her with one."

It was then that Anoushka saw the great man in action.

His assistants hurried with silks, tulles, velvets, brocades, cloth of silver, lace, gauze, all of which he threw casually over Anoushka's shoulder, held them against her waist, or tried them in all the colours of the rainbow against her skin.

Then he was scribbling sketches on pieces of paper, calling for more and yet more satins, spangles, fringes, tassels, and feathers, until Anoushka felt she would be swamped by her clothing and left with no individuality of her own.

It was the Duke who inspected the sketches, listened to Mr. Worth, and decided what should be made.

Only when they drove away and Anoushka felt as if she must breathe deeply to resuscitate herself did she begin to laugh.

"How dare you laugh at the most acclaimed man in all Paris!" the Duke said with mock severity.

"He was so funny!" Anouskha said. "All those people running round him like busy little ants, and he giving orders as if he were creating the world rather than a gown."

"You are committing *lèse-majesté,*" the Duke complained. "If he were aware of it, he might refuse to design for you, and then where would you be?"

"Perhaps like Eve, looking for fig-leaves, but in the Bois rather than the Garden of Eden," Anoushka replied, and the Duke joined in her laughter.

He took her to luncheon at the Pre Catelan in the Bois becuase he wanted to see what she would make of the beautiful *Amazones* who galloped between the Porte

Dauphine and the Champs des Courses, and stopped there to refresh themselves and exchange gossip.

Until he arrived there he had forgotten that he knew so many people in Paris that it was inevitable that he should find himself surrounded by friends and that Anoushka would be the object of their intense curiosity.

He introduced a number of people to her, then he quickly moved her away to a secluded table under the shelter of one of the trees.

"We will have a very light luncheon," he said, "because tonight I intend to take you to a Restaurant where there is no dancing but where the food is superlative and those who dine there think of little else."

"I think that food must be very important to the French," Anoushka remarked.

"That is true," the Duke agreed. "They have in fact two national passions which absorb them to the exclusion of all else."

"What is the second one?" Anoushka asked.

"Love," the Duke replied.

She looked at him in surprise.

"Do you mean that they think about it almost as if it were a subject of study?"

"To the Frenchman it is an Art, as important as painting, music, sculpture, or food."

"There must be a great deal to learn about love."

"A Frenchman takes a lifetime to be proficient in it."

The Duke saw that Anoushka was puzzling over what he had said. Then three people came up to the table with exclamations of delight at seeing him.

Leading them was an Englishwoman with whom the Duke had had a fiery, tempestuous affair which had ended only when her husband, who was a Diplomat at the Court of St. James's, had been moved to another country.

La Comtesse de Portales, as she was now, was still exceedingly beautiful and was well aware of it.

Her red hair and slanting green eyes had held many men captive, and the two Frenchmen who accompanied her were both friends of the Duke and were delighted to see him.

"I intended to call on you this afternoon," the *Comtesse* said, "to offer you my congratulations and of course my good wishes for your happiness. You know, dear Raven, that I want you to be happy."

She looked up into the Duke's eyes in a manner which said without words that she thought it was very unlikely he would find that elusive goal except with her.

"You are even more beautiful than I remember, Madelaine," the Duke said courteously, raising her hand to his lips.

She smiled at him intimately before he said:

"Let me present you to my wife. Anoushka, *la Comtesse* de Portales, who was an irreparable loss to England when she left it."

Anoushka curtseyed, and as the two men were shaking hands with the Duke and congratulating him on his marriage, the *Comtesse* looked her up and down in a manner that was very different from the way she had looked at the Duke.

Then as if she decided to make something very clear she said:

"I was most surprised to hear of the Duke's marriage. He has been a very close and very dear friend of mine, and I thought he might have informed me of his intentions."

Anoushka looked at the woman with interest, and she thought she could understand why the Duke admired her.

She was certainly extremely beautiful, and yet instinctively Anoushka felt that beneath the surface she was not a good woman and that the attitude she had towards her was unpleasant.

"You must visit my house," the *Comtesse* continued, "and you must not mind, Duchess, if your husband and I have a great deal to say to each other. As I have already told you, he is a very, very dear friend."

There was an acid note in the *Comtesse*'s voice that Anoushka did not miss.

Then she realised that this lady was angry because the Duke had married her.

Quite suddenly she thought the reason was very obvious.

"Were you my husband's mistress, *Madame*?" she enquired.

The other woman was turned to stone and for a moment there was silence from sheer astonishment. Then she said furiously:

"How dare you ask me such a thing! I have never been so insulted in my whole life!"

Her voice rose as she spoke, and the Duke and the two men talking to him turned their heads to see what was occurring.

Then as the *Comtesse* stalked away, her bustle moving behind her like the tail-feathers of an angry turkey, the two men murmured their apologies and followed after her.

The Duke looked at Anoushka.

"What happened? What did you say to upset her?" he enquired.

"I . . . I am sorry if what I said was . . . wrong," Anoushka answered.

As if overcome by what had happened, she sat down again at the table and the Duke did the same.

"But what upset her?" he asked again.

Anoushka looked towards the Restaurant where she could see the *Comtesse* speaking angrily and waving her hands about and insisting on leaving while the gentlemen tried to persuade her to stay.

"I had no idea that what I said would . . . make her so . . .cross," she said, "or . . . that it was . . . rude."

"What did you say?" the Duke insisted.

"She told me how much you . . . meant to each other, and

I . . . asked her if she had been your . . . mistress,"
Anoushka said in a low voice.

As she spoke she looked at the Duke pleadingly, begging
him to understand that she had not meant to be rude or
insulting, but had merely thought it was the logical explanation of the way the *Comtesse* was speaking of him.

For the moment the Duke looked stern, then quite unexpectedly he laughed.

"You are . . . not angry?" Anoushka asked.

"It was my fault," he said. "I can understand how this all
evolved from our conversation about *Madame* de Pompadour. I should have warned you never to call a woman a
man's mistress to her face, as it is certainly not a compliment, especially when she is a lady who, if she has love-
affairs, tries to do so very secretly and everybody pretends
to know nothing about them!"

"But was she your mistress?"Anoushka asked.

"That is a question which you must understand I cannot
answer, because it is dishonourable for a man to betray a
woman's secrets or to mention her name in public."

"Or to his wife?"

The Duke felt that once again he had stepped into a
maze.

Only last night he had been telling Anoushka there
should be no secrets between them, and now he was saying
that where he was concerned there must must be one.

He found himself wondering how he had ever gone
through life until now without becoming so involved in the
inevitable laws of social behaviour and finding them so
difficult to explain.

Then as he was silent Anoushka said:

"I am sorry . . . very sorry to have . . . done anything . . .
wrong, but I did warn you that because I am so . . . ignorant
I was not the . . . right sort of wife for you to marry."

"What you do or what you say at the moment does not
concern our marriage," the Duke said. "You might just as

well say your School is a bad one and you should not be there because you got one lesson wrong. What actually is wrong is the inadequacy of your teacher."

Anoushka smiled and it swept the worry from her eyes.

"I do not think even your worst enemy could call you inadequate," she said, "and you are, I know, a very clever man."

"And you think you are capable of judging me?" the Duke asked sarcastically.

"I can only compare you with the other people I have met, the teachers who came to the Convent specially and told me they were the best in Paris. And of course we were instructed by some of the most important Priests in France. Even the Cardinal called on us once or twice a year."

"So you felt you could appraise their talents and intelligence when you were gaining their commendation," the Duke remarked cynically.

He knew as he spoke that he had upset her, and as she looked away from him across the garden he said quickly:

"Believe me, Anoushka, I am pleased and honoured that you should admire my intellect. It is something I want you to do."

"I-it was . . . presumptuous of me to comment or to compare you with other people."

The Duke realised that she was far too perceptive not to have realised that it had flashed through his mind that it was an impertinence and that a young and supremely ignorant girl who had lived only in a Convent should criticise him even favourably.

Then he realised that from her point of view it was the greatest compliment she could pay him.

It was a fact that although she had been incarcerated between four walls, she had nevertheless studied under people who were high in their own professions and who, unlike the majority of his friends, used their brains.

He had no idea as he was thinking about her that

Anoushka was reading his thoughts, and after a moment she said:

"Now that you are forgiving me, I am glad . . . so very glad. Please . . .. do not let what I have done . . . . spoil our luncheon . . . and I promise I will never say such a thing again."

She looked so lovely as she was pleading with him that the Duke thought he would have to have been made of granite not to respond wholeheartedly to what she said.

"Forget the whole episode," he said. "It is of no importance."

"But your friend . . . the *Comtesse*."

"I will send her some flowers and an apology," the Duke said, "and there is no need for me to see her again."

Anoushka looked at him quickly.

"But perhaps you want to . . . and if so, I could stay at home and you could go to her house . . . alone."

"I have no wish to do that," the Duke replied, and realised to his surprise that it was the truth.

After luncheon they drove round the Bois. Then as it was very hot the Duke took Anoushka back to the house and they sat on the terrace overlooking the garden and felt the faint cool breeze coming from the Seine.

"It is cooler here," Anoushka said as the servants brought them long drinks of fresh lime-juice.

"Personally, I find it unpleasantly hot," the Duke said. "Tomorrow we will leave for the South of France, where it will be hotter still, but there will be breezes from the sea and we will have nothing to do but enjoy the sunshine until my yacht arrives."

"Your yacht?" Anoushka questioned.

"I have sent for it to come to Nice," The Duke said, "and I think perhaps we will cruise down the Mediterranean, stopping at any country that interests you."

He watched her face as he went on:

"There is Italy, Sicily, Greece, and of course if we were

very adventurous we could go on to Constantinople and into the Black Sea.

He thought Anoushka drew in her breath, but he was not sure.

Then quickly, before he could say any more, she said:

"Please, let us do that. It is something I would like above all things, and I am never sea-sick."

The Duke thought this was definitely an inadvertent clue about her secret past, but he made no comment except to say:

"The gowns from Worth will have to follow us, but I think you will find that one or two will be ready tomorrow, and I have already ordered some more from the dressmakers from whom I bought the one you have on."

"I am afraid I am costing you a lot of money."

"You have forgotten that you could pay for them yourself."

"Of course! I have forgotten, because at the Convent we never had any money! But there is something much more important I must do."

"What is that?" the Duke asked.

"You said that I could buy you a present which I could pay for myself, and I want it to be a very, very expensive one, because you have given me so much."

"Not as much as I intend to give you," the Duke replied. "I am finding it fascinating to dress a woman 'from scratch,' so to speak, and one who is content to let me have my own way."

He might have guessed, he thought after he had spoken, that Anoushka would not let such a remark pass.

"I think what you are saying, *Monseigneur*," she said, " is that you have dressed other women in the past. Were they your . . ."

The word "mistresses" hovered on her lips, but she bit it back.

The Duke smiled to himself.

He wondered how many dozens of gowns he had been coaxed into paying for by the women who had granted him their favors.

There had also been furs — ermines and sables — and jewels, so many necklaces, ear-rings, bracelets, and brooches that he had lost count.

He was well aware that the women to whom he had made love, whether they were Ladies of Quality or *demi-mondaines,* thought that because he was so rich that it was only right that he should pay for the privilege to the utmost that they could extract from him.

Of course they gave him presents in return, but always things that were small and of no intrinsic value.

It was something new to have a woman wish to pay back what he was spending in the same generous way that he gave.

"What I wanted to do," Anoushka said, "was to give you something you do not have already. But this would be impossible if all your houses are as perfect as this one. But I have thought of something that I could give you, if you would help me choose it."

"What is that?" the Duke asked.

"A horse," Anoushka said. "The horses you have here in Paris are very fine, and from what you said when you were talking about your stables in England, I think those you have there must be finer still."

He looked at her in surprise as she went on:

"Could you please choose a really fantastic horse, one that is so good and so fine that it will win lots of races? Then if I could pay for it, I feel it would bear comparison with the diamonds and gowns which you have given to me."

The Duke was amused and rather touched.

"Thank you, Anoushka," he said. "Nobody else is likely to give me a horse for a weddig present, and I would like it above all things."

Anoushka clapped her hands together like a child.

"When can we choose it? And where?"

"As soon as we get back to England," the Duke said. "There is a Sales-Room in London called Tattersall's, where I buy quite a number of my horses. Or we can visit some of the Breeders and see what they have to offer."

Anoushka's eyes were shining as she said:

"I was not wrong! I thought that was what you would like. I am so glad!"

"We will choose it together," the Duke said. "And now there is another thing I want to ask you."

"What is that?"

"Can you ride?"

"Not well enough to ride with you," she said in a low voice. "I . . . used to think I rode well . . . but that was a long time . . . ago."

"You mean you rode before you went to the Convent?"

The Duke realised that he had caught her off her guard, and for a moment she did not know what to say.

Then, as if she felt there was no harm in admitting that it was the truth, she said:

"Yes . . . but I am sure riding is . . . something one does not . . . forget."

"We will soon find out," the Duke said, "but I would rather you started at home on my own horses than here in Paris."

"Yes . . . of course," Anoushka said quickly. "It would be very humiliating if I fell off in the Bois where there are so many people . . . and please . . . will you teach me yourself?"

"Of course," the Duke agreed. "And I am sure, from the way you move, that you will be a very fine rider."

"It is something I am sure all Englishmen do well."

The Duke was aware that she was thinking of her father, and he said:

"I hope you will always think so, and as an Englishwoman, Anoushka, and as my wife, you must learn to hunt, for it is something I very much enjoy in the winter, and I have my own pack of fox-hounds."

"Explain to me, explain to me exactly what that means," Anoushka said. "I did know once, but I may have forgotten."

By the time they went back for dinner, the Duke thought he had never spent a more unusual and intriguing afternoon.

He was beginning to find it fascinating to learn the extreme contrasts in Anoushka's knowledge. In some subjects, the academic ones, she knew as much as he did, if not more, but in others there were voids of ignorance, and because she demanded it he tried to fill them.

He found himself understanding why parents liked to answer the questions their children asked them, to read to them, and to instruct them.

But Anoushka was not a child, and she had a rapier-like intelligence which made her never miss a point and a memory which he found so retentive that everything he said to her was remembered and catalogued for future use.

When she came into the Salon before dinner he thought it ridiculous, with her looks, for her to concentrate so insistently on her mind, or for him to do so.

Every time she changed her gown it seemed to him she took on a different beauty as the colours themselves were reflected differently in her eyes.

The *Coiffeur* was also trying out different styles on her hair, and the Duke found it difficult to say which he preferred.

Tonight she was wearing a gown of silver and white which he had bought because it seemed to him appropriately bridal.

The silver was echoed, he thought, in the strange silver streaks in her hair, and round her neck instead of diamonds she wore a necklace of large Oriental pearls he had sent to her room before dinner, which were glowingly translucent against the whiteness of her skin.

She looked very young, very ethereal, and almost like a sprite arising from the Seine rather than a Duchess of the Social World.

As she crossed the room towards him her eyes were watching the expression on his face. He knew she was wanting his approval and was nervous in case there was something wrong with her gown.

She stood waiting for him to speak, and after a moment he said:

"You look very lovely! Is that what you want me to tell you, or has your mirror done so already?"

She gave a little laugh before she said:

"How do you know I looked at my reflection hoping it would tell me the truth?"

"That is what every woman does when she wears a new gown, and if you had not liked what you saw, you would have changed into something else, and I would have had to wait for you."

"I would not have dared to be late," Anoushka replied, "but I would have been upset if you had not approved."

"When we have been married a little longer you will grow tired of my compliments," the Duke said lightly.

Anoushka shook her head.

"They are very, very exciting for me because I have never had any before."

"I suppose that is true," the Duke conceded. "That is why, if for no other reason, you will find it amusing to be with men rather than shut away with nothing but women!"

"Do all men pay women compliments?" she asked.

"I promise you will receive a great many before you are very much older," the Duke said.

His prophecy very soon proved to be true, because when they arrived at the Grand Vevour, a small but very exclusive Restaurant where he had taken Anoushka to dine, two of his French friends hurried to their table as soon as they were seated.

When the Duke presented them to Anoushka they kissed her hand and, speaking fluent English, paid her compliments which made her look at them wide-eyed.

"How can Raven, who has always beaten us in every race, have carried off yet another prize so alluring, so exquisite," one asked, "without our even being able to compete for it?"

"Are you saying that I am the prize?" Anoushka asked ingenuously.

"Of course, Duchess, although 'prize' is an inadequate word. You are a star glittering out of reach, the moon for which every man yearns, and the sun which Raven has now made exclusively his when you should really shine your radiance for the benefit of all mankind."

They said a great deal more before they went back to their own table, and when they were gone Anoushka said with laughter in her voice:

"You were quite right. I enjoy compliments, and I hope I have many, many more."

"The two gentlemen you have just met are unusually poetic," the Duke said drily. "An Englishman will simply tell you you are a 'good sport' and a 'fine figure of a woman'! And even then they will feel they are being over-effusive!"

Anoushka laughed. Then she asked:

"And what compliments do you pay to the ladies you admire and . . . love?"

"That is something I must not tell you," the Duke replied.

"It is a secret?"

"Not exactly a secret, but indiscreet, and something that would make the average wife jealous."

There was silence. Then Anoushka said:

"You mean . . . that if you . . . admire another woman . . . I should be jealous?"

"It is what most women would be."

"But . . . why?"

"Because I am your husband, and I am supposed to be interested only in my wife, and of course be faithful to her."

"And was the lady we met today not married when you were, as she said, 'very close friends'?"

The Duke thought that once again he had been "hoist with his own petard" and was relieved that for the moment, while they were served with one of the exotic courses he had ordered and the waiter hovered over them, it was impossible to speak intimately.

But he might have guessed that what he had said was being turned over in Anoushka's mind, and when the meal was finished and there was only the coffee left in front of them and a glass of brandy for the Duke, she said:

"Could I ask you a question?"

"Of course," he answered.

"Now that we are married, if you see a woman you think beautiful and attractive . . . and want to say loving things to her . . . am I to pretend that I do not . . . know what is happening?"

"Let us hope it is something that will not happen," the Duke replied, "but if it does, it should be something that is kept secret from you, and certainly it would be beneath your condescension to interfere."

"But you said that most wives would be jealous."

"I think all women are jealous of a rival," the Duke said evasively.

There was silence. Then Anoushka said:

"Then, supposing I listened to compliments from another man and found him interesting . . . would you pretend not to notice?"

"Certainly not!" the Duke said sharply. "That is something that must not happen, and as my wife you must behave decently and with propriety, which means there would be no other men in your life except me."

Once again he was thinking of Cleodel as he spoke, and

he was sure that if he had married her she would have continued her affair with Jimmy.

The whole idea disgusted him, and without his meaning to his voice had sharpened and he answered Anoushka almost ferociously.

Then as he finished speaking he thought he might have frightened her and he should try to somehow soothe her feelings if she was upset. But before he could speak she said in a quiet voice:

"That does not seem fair!"

"Fair?" the Duke queried.

"For a man to be entitled to do something, but not a woman. Surely if it is right for the husband it must be right for his wife, and vice-versa."

The Duke realised she was arguing for the sake of it and not because she felt personally involved.

At the same time, he thought, seeing what he had suffered with Cleodel, he should make things clear from the very beginning.

He took a sip of his brandy before he said:

"There is something I want to tell you, Anoushka."

"What is that?"

"When I came to the Convent I was seeking a wife who would be different from all the other women I have ever known."

"In what way?"

"I asked my sister to find me a girl who, because she had been brought up as a Novice, would be pure and untouched. It was then that she suggested you."

There was a long silence. Then Anoushka said:

"I think . . . what you are saying is . . . that the women and girls you have met outside the Convent, in the world in which you . . . live, were neither of those things."

This, the Duke thought, was rather sweeping, and he prevaricated by answering:

"It is difficult to be sure, and although one must always

believe that they have been brought up to keep themselves chaste until they marry, there is always the chance that they have been tempted into an indiscetion."

"You mean they might have met men about whom their parents knew nothing, and who would . . . kiss them?"

The Duke understood how this fitted in with the conversation he had had with Anoushka earlier, and he said:

"That is what I meant, for girls, even in the most aristocratic families, have for instance Riding-Masters and meet other men employed by their fathers. There are also men who are unscrupulous and find very young girls attractive."

Once again his voice sharpened as he thought that that was what Jimmy had felt about Cleodel.

"You said you did not want to tell me what had happened in the past," Anoushka said in a low voice, "but I think you have been hurt . . . wounded . . . and it is something you . . . have to forget if you are to be . . . happy again."

The Duke could find no words in which to answer her. He only knew that she had an extraordinary power of perception where he was concerned, and it would be impossible for him to refute anything she had said.

Instead he changed the subject, talking about the Palais Royal, in which the Grand Vevour was situated, describing what it had been like when it was the private house of the *Duc* d'Orleans, and how overnight he became a very rich man when he turned it into a place of amusement with Casinos and Restaurants.

Anoushka listened wide-eyed. Then she said:

"Did the men in those days come here with their wives?"

"Certainly not!" the Duke replied. "Ladies never go to such places, and when we leave Paris for England, Anoushka, you will not be able to dine in a Restaurant."

"Why not?"

"Because it is something which a woman in your position, what we call a 'lady,' cannot do."

"But there are Restaurants in which you may dine?"

"Yes," the Duke admitted.

"With a women who would be your mistress?"

"Speaking generally and not personally," he said, "the answer is 'yes.' "

"It seems to me that the women I am not supposed to talk about have a far more amusing time than I will."

"That has been said before," the Duke replied, "but it depends what you call amusement. You, Anoushka, being a Duchess, have a great social position. You will entertain all the most interesting and important people in the land. They will stay with us in the country and dine with us in London."

He saw that she was listening intently, and went on:

"People will look up to you and admire you, especially on my Estate where at Ravenstock alone I employ two thousand people. They will expect you to be interested in them and to look after them."

"How should I do that?"

"My mother would call at their cottages. She also wished to be told when anybody was ill. She gave a party for them at Christmas, and I think I am not exaggerating when I say that everybody loved her."

"And you think they will love me?"

"I am sure of it."

"And do they love you?"

"I hope so. I think perhaps they respect and admire me, and know that I will always be just and generous in anything I do which concerns them."

The Duke smiled as he continued:

"The women I do not wish you to talk about cannot have any of that, nor can they have children who can bear my name, and my eldest son will inherit my title."

There was just a touch of satisfaction in the Duke's voice.

For the first time he began to think, because he was describing it to Anoushka, that he would really enjoy having a son, or sons. He would teach them how to shoot, how to ride, and to enjoy his horses and Estates as he enjoyed them himself.

"If we had a child," Anoushka said in a very small voice, "we would never have to part with it?"

"Never!" the Duke said positively.

He knew she was thinking that she had been parted from her parents, and now he was concentrating on the mystery of why she had been brought to the Convent and abandoned there.

Because he felt it was better not to ask her any questions he said:

"Our children will be with us when they are small, but the boys will have to go away to School. They will of course always come home for the holidays, and we can visit them when they are at Eton and see that they are always well looked after and have everything they want."

He paused before he went on:

"I am thinking that what you said is right, Anoushka. It is funny, and perhaps wrong, for a man to have so many houses in which to live by himself when they should be filled with children who laugh as you laugh, play, and find life exciting."

"If you can give me children," Anoushka said, "why can you not give children to the ladies whose names I am not allowed to mention?"

The Duke thought this was one of the questions he had anticipated would arise sooner or later, but once again he evaded it.

"I think we should leave now," he said. "Would you like to go somewhere else, or would you prefer to drive home with the carriage open? I think we should go to bed soon, as we are leaving early tomorrow morning."

"Yes, of course," Anoushka agreed.

They drove back under the stars and as she looked up at them as she had done the previous night the Duke had the strange feeling that she had for the moment forgotten his very existence.

He knew that any other woman would have been nestling against him, holding his hand under the rug, and waiting for him to whisper words of love in a low passionate voice.

But Anoushka sat upright and her head was tilted back as they drove in silence until they reached the Champs Élysées.

Then, as if she suddenly remembered him, she turned to look at the Duke and say:

"Are you really going to bed now, or do you intend to look for your friends, perhaps in the places you will not take me?"

The Duke was startled not so much by what she said but because once again she was reading his thoughts.

He had in fact been deliberating whether he should drop into Maxim's, knowing that because it was the most fashionable Restaurant in Paris, he would doubtless know most of the men in the whole room.

The women, who would be the smartest, most fashionable *demi-mondaines* in the whole Capital, would welcome him eagerly.

Then because he felt that if he went to Maxim's his presence there when he was on his honeymoon would reflect on Anoushka, and also because, surprisingly, he really had no wish for the superficial gaiety of Maxim's, he replied quite truthfully:

"No, Anoushka, I am coming to bed, and like you I shall think of all the interesting things there will be to do when we reach the South. I am sure you have a thousand questions to ask me, for which I shall have to find the answers."

"You do not mind answering them?" Anoushka asked anxiously.

"I promise you it is something I shall enjoy, although I am quite nervous of displaying my ignorance."

Anoushka laughed.

"That you will never do, and you have to teach me very quickly so that I shall not make mistakes like the one I made today."

"I told you to forget it," the Duke said firmly.

"I am trying to," Anoushka replied, "but I know that even if you have forgiven me, the lady to whom I spoke will hate me, and that is wrong because I am your wife."

"And as your husband I can tell you quite truthfully that it does not worry me and is really of no importance," the Duke said.

They stepped out of the carriage, and because it was after midnight the Duke did not go into the Salon to have another drink, but walked up the stairs beside Anoushka.

Their bedrooms were side by side, with a communicating-door which had not been opened.

They stopped outside the first door, which was Anoushka's.

"Thank you very much for such a delicious dinner and for talking to me," she said.

"It is I who should be thanking you," the Duke replied. 'I have found our conversations very interesting and certainly original."

"You mean it would have been different if you had been with anybody else?"

"Very different," the Duke said with a smile, "and that is what makes knowing you so unusual, and I think I might almost use the word 'intriguing.' "

"So you have not been . . . bored?"

"Of course not! And I can say this quite honestly: there has not been a moment since we have been together when I have felt in the least bored or had the slightest wish to be anywhere else except with you."

Her smile was dazzling. Then she gave a little laugh.

"Now you are talking like a Frenchman," she said. "I thought you told me that the English never pay compliments."

"I am the exception."

"Of course," she replied. "And . . . please . . . because I like hearing them, will you pay me lots and lots of them and forget you are English?"

"Only if they are truthful," he said.

"I shall know if they are," she replied. "But actually any compliment is better than none."

The Duke laughed, and taking her hand in his raised it to his lips.

"Let me tell you one more," he said. "I like the quickness of your brain and I enjoy your laughter."

He kissed her hand, his lips warm on the softness of her skin.

As he did so he wondered if he should kiss her lips. Then he thought it was far too soon, and he remembered that Anoushka had said she had no wish to be touched.

He raised his head and, still holding her hand, he said:

"Good-night, Anoushka. Sleep well. There are new excitements tomorrow which I shall look forward to."

"It will be very . . . very exciting for me too."

She spoke eagerly but lightly and took her hand from the Duke's.

Then she smiled at him as she opened the door of her bedroom.

He waited until the last frill of her bustle disappeared before he walked towards his own room.

He had the feeling that he was losing or missing something that he should not let escape him.

Then he told himself he was just being fanciful.

At the same time, as his valet helped him undress, he was thinking of Anoushka.

Chapter Six

AS THE yacht steamed into the Black Sea, the Duke was watching Anoushka's face, feeling sure that she was showing a significantly different kind of excitement in her eyes.

Intent on finding clues to her past, he had found one of curious significance the moment they had arrived at Nice.

They had stepped out of the special carriage attached to the train to find that as usual the Courier who had gone ahead of them had arranged for the Duke's own carriage drawn by his own horses to be waiting outside the station.

The morning sunshine made it imperative to have the carriage open, but there was a fringed linen canopy to protect them from the sun.

As they drove away, Anoushka had glimpses of the blue sea. Then after they had passed through the town and started to climb the hills above Nice to where the private Villas were situated, the Duke heard her suddenly give a gasp.

"Cypress trees!" she exclaimed in a rapt voice.

The words were spoken under her breath, and yet he heard them and saw the expression of surprise in her eyes.

Silhouetted against the sky were a number of cypress trees pointing like fingers towards the heavens, and he knew as they drove on that her eyes were on them rather than on the Alps in the far distance.

The Duke had by now learnt not to ask searching questions which embarrassed Anoushka because she felt she could not reply to them.

Instead he merely watched her, and he found himself intrigued and interested in a manner which he began to think was different from anything he had ever experienced before.

When he was alone he found himself wondering why cypress trees should have such an importance for her.

They were very familiar in France and Italy. Then suddenly a thought came to him which he felt was very illuminating.

He remembered that when he had visited Russia he had read a great deal about the history of the country and its Tsars.

Now at the back of his memory he recalled that one book had told him that the tall, lofty, romantic cypress trees had first been planted by the Empress Catherine on her journey with Potemkin to her Southern possessions.

From these trees were grafted all the many cypress groves and avenues which over the years had come to be typical of the Crimean landscape.

More especially was Odessa connected with cypress trees.

The Duke had felt as elated as if he had won a hard race or defeated an opponent in the boxing-ring.

"We will go to Odessa!" he thought to himself, but he was too wise to say so to Anoushka. He would let it be a surprise.

After they had spent only two days in his Villa, the Duke so impatient to put his theory to the proof that early the next day they sailed for Villefranche as their first port-of-call.

It was a brilliant morning which soon became very hot, but they found the sea breeze pleasantly refreshing.

Anoushka was as delighted with the yacht as she had been thrilled, almost like a child with a new doll's-house, by the Duke's private coach on the train.

From little things she said, the Duke knew that she had been in a ship before, but obviously not a private one.

There was no hurry and they sailed slowly down the coast of Italy, occasionally stopping in some small port to go ashore and look at the local sights.

The Duke had no wish at the moment to take Anoushka to Rome or Naples, and he thought even Pompeii could wait for another time.

It was only when they reached the Greek Islands that he recognised this as a desire to be alone with Anoushka and not share her with the crowds and sightseers.

Then he admitted to himself that he was falling in love.

At first he could not believe it possible. He had been so sure after leaving England, with his hatred of Cleodel distorting his whole outlook, that never again would he care for a woman or let one in any way encroach on his heart.

And yet, as he watched Anoushka, as he listened to her questions and strove to answer them, he knew that he found everything about her entrancing.

It was not only her beauty which attracted him but something else that was very different.

He thought now that he should have become aware of the change in his feelings when, the day before they had left Nice, the Courier he had sent to London arrived to report what had occurred after the announcement of his marriage had appeared in the newspapers.

The man had described the astonishment amongst the Duke's friends, the scenes which the Earl of Sedgewick had made at Ravenstock House, and the difficulty Mr. Matthews was having with him and a great number of other callers.

Although the Duke could visualise it all vividly, he found surprisingly that it did not give him any elation or the satisfaction that he had expected.

Quite suddenly it did not seem to matter very much what had been said or done, and England was far away.

Even then, he would not face them for this reason, and it was only when the yacht was steaming towards Constantinople that he admitted that he loved Anoushka in a way he had never loved before, though he was puzzlingly uncertain as to what he could do about it.

In all his considerable experience he had never been with

a woman for so long who had not fallen in love with him.

Because he himself was now genuinely in love, he could not blind himself to the truth, nor could he pretend that Anoushka's feelings were anything but those of a pupil for a much-admired teacher.

She listened intently to everything he said, with her huge eyes on his face and with a serenity which he admired and which he had never found except in his sister, Marguerite.

When they discussed academic subjects, Anoushka showed remarkable powers of concentration, and when they argued together the Duke felt he must polish up his brain to keep his end up, let alone defeat her.

On other subjects she was so adorably childlike that he felt at times it would be a mistake to awaken her to a very different point of view.

And yet he could not disguise from himself that he desired her as a woman and that it was not a child who made the blood throb in his temples, his heart beat alarmingly, and a desire rise that seemed at times to be almost uncontrollable.

Then, because the Duke had long practised strict self-discipline, he acted his part with what he told himself was an admirable restraint.

Only at times he wondered frantically whether he would be able to last one month, let alone three, without taking Anoushka in his arms.

But he had given Marguerite his word of honour, and he could break it only if Anoushka asked him to make love to her.

As she had not the slightest idea what this meant, and did not think of him as a desirable man, he thought despairingly that it could never happen and it was a barrier between them that he saw no way of demolishing.

"What am I to do?" he asked himself helplessly at night after Anoushka had gone to her own cabin.

As he could not sleep, he would stand on deck looking at

the stars overhead and thinking that he was more lonely than he had ever been in his whole life.

He thought of the women who had tried by every trick that was known to attract his attention, who had contrived in a thousand different ways to get him to themselves.

He would never have believed that he could be in a position where he could not attract one young girl or bring even an expression of affection to her eyes or to her lips.

"Now that you have seen something of the world, what do you think of it?" he asked Anoushka.

He was genuinely curious to hear her answer.

They had by now sailed past Constantinople without stopping there, gone up the Bosporus and into the Black Sea, and now were sitting comfortably side by side on deck-chairs, after an excellent luncheon cooked by one of the Duke's most experienced Chefs.

He thought that Anoushka in a white gown made of muslin looked like the wild-flowers they had seen growing on the Greek Islands and which she had said must have sprung from the footsteps of the gods.

"What do you expect me to feel when everything you have shown me is so beautiful?" Anoushka replied. "When I was at the Convent I used to try to make pictures for myself of the places I read about, and they became part of my dreams. Now I think I must be dreaming."

"Are there any people in your dreams?"

"Sometimes."

"Real people?"

The Duke thought she hesitated before she replied again:

"Sometimes."

"Do you think in the future I shall ever be in your dreams?"

He mocked at himself as he asked the question, knowing it was one he had never asked before, because all other women with whom he had talked would have already told him plainly that all their dreams included him.

"How do I know until I do dream of you?" Anoushka asked in a soft voice which the Duke had long recognised as entirely impersonal.

"I shall be extremely piqued if I am not in your dreams," he said lightly. "After all, I am the only man you know."

"Do most women dream of a man?" Anoushka asked.

"Invariably," the Duke replied. "Women do not feel complete when they are alone. They feel that they need a man with them, not only in real life but also when they are asleep."

He paused, and when she did not answer he added:

"The man in their dreams is the one they are always seeking in their hearts."

"Do they want to marry him?"

"Of course," the Duke replied.

'Then what happens when they are married?"

He smiled to himself as he thought this was a question he might have expected.

"Ideally," he replied after a minute's thought, "a married woman will dream of her husband, but I am afraid that does not always happen."

"But you said," Anoushka answered, "that a married woman, if she behaves correctly, can never be interested in any man except her husband."

"That is what a husband expects, and what I would expect of you."

"But you will not be able to control my dreams," Anoushka said, "and if I dream of somebody else I shall be the only person to know I have dreamt something wrong."

"I should be very upset and hurt if I thought you were dreaming of another man," the Duke said, choosing his words with care.

"Then I will certainly keep it a secret," she said, "and I

suppose you are allowed to dream of any woman you like and I must not be upset or hurt!"

"Would you be?" the Duke asked.

It was a leading question, but he had to ask it.

Anoushka was looking out to sea, and he knew she was thinking seriously over what he had asked her. Then she gave one of her unexpected lilting laughs.

"This is a very funny conversation," she said. "How can we be so foolish as to worry about our dreams? Mine are sometimes very complicated. Last night I dreamt I was flying over the sea. . . "

"Alone?" the Duke enquired.

"I think so," she replied. "It was a lovely feeling, sweeping through the air like a bird, and I was disappointed when I woke up."

The Duke gave a sigh.

Once again the conversation had veered away from himself, and he knew Anoushka was not thinking of him in any way except as a companion who was a mine of information.

"You have not forgotten," she said, "that you promised that when we reached the Black Sea you would take me sailing? I have never sailed in a small boat, and I think perhaps it would be almost like flying."

"We will sail in an hour's time, when it is a little cooler," the Duke promised.

He had already given the Captain instructions that they were to anchor in one of the small bays along the coast.

He did not want to arrive at Odessa until early one morning when he intended there should be plenty of time for him to watch Anoushka's reaction when she first saw the cypress trees, the spires, and the towers of the city ahead of them.

He would take her ashore, and perhaps then he would find out the secret which she had kept hidden for so long and which she had still not made up her mind to confide to him.

Perhaps then, the Duke told himself optimistically, when that barrier between them fell, she would feel herself closer to him than she was at the moment, and the restrictions would fall one by one.

He was watching her while he thought it over, and she was looking exceedingly lovely.

He suddenly felt such a desire to touch her that only years of self-discipline prevented him from putting out his hands, pulling her to her feet, and taking her into his arms.

It had been an agony, and yet a joy, when a week ago in a small harbour in the South of Italy, where they had rested for the night, a Band consisting of two violins and a man who beat tambourenes, a cymbal, or rang bells played on the side of the quay.

They had been in the Saloon with the port-holes open to let in the night breeze.

Anoushka had run to one of them exclaiming with delight not only at the music but at the strange way in which the musicians were dressed.

Then the Duke had said:

"I think this is an excellent opportunity for me to show you how to dance."

As he had expected, she learnt very quickly, and was so light on her feet that he felt he was dancing with some mythical being rather than with a woman.

He danced her round and round the Saloon, and when the music stopped she clapped her hands in delight and begged for more.

When she became quite proficient and could follow his steps without difficulty, the Duke drew her a little closer and was aware how much the nearness of her slim body affected him.

Then as another dreamy waltz came to an end and they were both still, he kept his arm round her and looked down into her eyes, upturned to his.

"Now we can dance together," he said.

His voice was very deep and had a passionate note which any experienced woman would have recognised.

"It is very exciting," Anoushka answered.

"Is it something you want to do again?"

"Of course! Again and again!" she replied. "Sometimes the girls at the Convent used to say they would like to dance, and those who had done so would try to describe what happened, but I never knew it would be like this!"

"Like what?" the Duke asked.

"Like being part of the music, so that I am not only listening to it but it is playing in my feet and in my body."

The Duke wanted to say: "You will feel the same about love," but he knew Anoushka would not understand.

Quite unselfconsciously she slipped away from his encircling arm and ran to the port-hole.

"We must wave to our little Band," she said, "and tell them how much we enjoyed their playing."

She waved as she spoke, and the Duke heard the men below them on the quay saying:

"Grazio, Signora, multo grazio!"

She turned to smile at the Duke and found he was very near to her.

"I should be saying the same thing," he said. *"Multo grazio, Signora!"*

She swept him a deep curtsey.

"Grazio, Signora," she replied.

Her eyes were laughing up at his but they did not hold the expression the Duke wished to see.

The sailors had now erected a mast on the lightest of the lifeboats with a bright red sail which was moving slightly in the wind.

Anoushka seated herself in the stern, the Duke took the tiller, and they began to move over the water.

"This is exciting!" she said. "How fast can we go?"

"That depends entirely on the wind," the Duke replied.

"The Captain thought it would be a little stronger later."

"I hope he is right."

She looked up at the sky, which was clear, although the sun was not so hot as it had been earlier in the day.

"What you have to do," the Duke said, "is to whistle. Every sailor knows he must whistle down the wind."

Anoushka laughed and pursed her lips.

The way she did so made the Duke long to kiss her, but while he was thinking about it he was busy adjusting the sail, letting the boom swing outwards so that they began to run a little quicker with the wind behind them.

"It works! It works!" Anoushka cried. "My whistle has brought the wind!"

It certainly seemed to have been effective, and the small boat increased its speed as the sail billowed out crimson against the deep blue of the water.

"Faster! Faster!" Anoushka kept crying, and the Duke managed by extremely skilful sailing to achieve what he thought to himself was quite an unusual speed.

They had been sailing for nearly half-an-hour when he looked up apprehensively and realised that the sun had vanished and instead of the pale, clear, translucent sky which he expected, it looked grey and somewhat turbulent.

The Duke looked over his shoulder.

Intent on pleasing Anoushka, he realised they had gone very much farther than he had intended, the yacht was out of sight, and he knew it would take them a long time to sail back.

"Keep your head down," he said to Anoushka, and swung the boom over to begin what he knew would require all his expertise as a yachtsman.

The Duke had done a great deal of sailing and was in fact exceedingly proficient at the sport, which he enjoyed.

Last year he had won a considerable number of races at Cowes in the Isle of Wight, and he always sailed against yachtsmen as experienced as himself when he was in the South of France.

Now he thought somewhat apprehensively that the weather was worsening rapidly, and knew he had made a mistake to come so far when both the wind and the sea in these parts could be unpredictable and treacherous.

"Is everything all right?" Anoushka asked.

"I am concentrating on getting us back to the yacht," he replied, not wishing to frighten her.

"The sea is getting rough."

"I had noticed that," he replied drily. "But you told me you were a good sailor."

"At least I was," she said, "but it would be very humiliating if you proved me wrong."

"One should never trust the Black Sea," the Duke replied, "even though it is my colour."

As he spoke, he wondered what Anoushka would think when she heard the crowds shouting: "Raven Black!" "Raven Black!" when his horses thundered towards the winning-post.

It always pleased him to find that he was popular with the racing-crowd, knowing they had an instinct that was seldom wrong as to whether a man was a good sportsman or not.

"Why is black your colour?" Anoushka asked.

"It seemed appropriate because my name is Raven."

"It does not suit you."

"Why should you think that?"

"Because if you resemble a bird at all, you are more like an eagle. I was watching two this morning when we went on deck after breakfast."

"I was watching them too," the Duke said, "but why do you think I resemble them?"

"They are not only magnificent, and they are called the King of the Birds, but they also seem imperious and disdainful of mere mortals, almost as if they belong to another world than ours."

"Do you think that is what I do?" the Duke asked.

"I think you are imperious, and I think too that while you take part in many different social spheres and activities, you could never belong to anything or anybody except yourself."

"Why should you think that?" he asked sharply.

Anoushka did not answer, and after he had adjusted a rope he said:

"I am waiting to hear your answer to my last question."

"It is difficult to explain to you, but I feel that you are sufficient in yourself and do not need, as most people do, others to inspire, guide, lead, or comfort you."

"I suppose what you are suggesting is flattering in a way," the Duke said. "At the same time, it would be very lonely if I took you literally."

"What I am really saying is that people are complementary to you, and not you to them. You do not need help as another man might."

The Duke wondered what Anoushka would say if he told her how much he needed her.

But he knew once again it was too soon — much too soon.

Then he realised that he had no time to think about Anoushka but must concentrate on sailing the boat in what was obviously going to be a dangerously rough sea.

The Duke remembered far too late that the storms in the Black Sea could blow up in a question of minutes, and this was what was happening now.

The wind increased so that he was forced to use all his strength to keep the boat on course, and the sea suddenly changed from rippling white-crested waves to large overpowering ones.

The Duke looked round and the nearest land appeared to consist of high cliffs, and to go near them would be to risk being dashed against the rocks.

Then just beyond them he saw what appeared to be a

small bay and beyond it a much lower coastline with trees coming almost down to the water's edge.

"We will make for the shore," he decided, and realised he had to shout the words at Anoushka to make her hear them.

She was sitting on the floor of the boat. She did not answer but gave him a smile that seemed to illuminate her face.

The Duke had no time to look at her again.

He was trying to work the boat by skilful tacking towards the shore, knowing he must avoid the cliffs and the rocks beneath them and make for the bay, or, if he missed that, the low-lying ground beyond it.

It was a slow process and an unpleasant one.

The wind almost tore the main sheet out of his hands. The boat was buffeted and swept from side to side, or else it pitched and tossed in a most unpleasant manner.

The Duke was fighting for every inch but making little headway. Then the rain came.

It came down torrentially, soaking them to the skin and creating a veil through which the Duke could not see. He could only hope blindly that he was still continuing in the right direction.

It was impossible to speak to Anoushka, nor could he do anything but attempt to keep the boat afloat while the rain teemed down with such violence that even through his yachting-coat it hurt his shoulders.

Then as he strove to look ahead, finding it hard to keep his eyes open against the force of the rain, the boat suddenly gave a violent jerk.

There was a scraping sound and the Duke knew that they had either run aground or hit a rock.

As he wondered frantically what he should do and how he should save Anoushka, a gust of wind that seemed almost like a whirlwind swung the boom round with a swiftness that took him by surprise.

It struck him with a violence against which he had no defence, and he was thrown, unconscious, to the bottom of the boat.

Then there was only darkness . . .

*

The Duke came back to consciousness as if from the end of a long tunnel . . .

First he was aware that he could think. A long way away there was a glimmer of light . . .

He felt as if he was struggling to breathe, struggling to live, and yet he could not move . . .

Then he heard a voice speaking, a voice he recognised, and he knew it was Anoushka's, but he could not understand what she was saying.

It puzzled him, and he thought for a moment that he had gone mad. Then he realised she was speaking in a strange language and knew it was Russian.

Her voice was still soft and clear, but occasionally she hesitated, as if she was trying to remember a word. Then she went on talking, and a man was answering her in the same language.

He seemed to have quite a lot to say in a voice that was slow and deep, and the Duke thought vaguely that he sounded educated.

Then he drifted away into unconsciousness.

*

When the Duke became conscious again there was only silence and he was aware of a pain at the back of his head.

Then he felt a sudden frantic fear that he had lost Anoushka.

He tried to open his eyes, but even while he was trying to do so, the darkness seemed to come towards him from the end of the tunnel, and he could not prevent it from over-powering him . . .

*

The Duke opened his eyes.

There was a bright warm light near him, and after a moment he realised it was a fire, the flames leaping high from large logs.

He tried to speak, to call Anoushka, and then she was beside him.

He stared at her, trying to focus on her face, and as he did so he realised that he was lying on a bed beside the fire.

It was a bed that was low on the ground, and Anoushka seemed to tower above him until she knelt down at his side.

"Can you speak?" she asked.

"Where — am — I?"

"You are all right, but I was afraid . . . so afraid . . . But you can . . . speak."

"Yes — I can — speak," the Duke replied in a louder tone.

"You are not hurt!"

She smiled at him, and he saw that her hair was loose, which puzzled him.

"What — happened?" he asked.

"We ran into a rock," she said, "but a kind and brave man saved us. He carried you from the boat. I was so . . . terrified you would . . . drown."

The Duke heard the pain in her voice and wanted to put out his hand towards her. As he tried to do so, he realised he was lying naked beneath some warm blankets.

As if she knew what he was thinking, Anoushka said:

"You were lucky, very, very lucky! The man who saved you is a Doctor. This is his holiday house, right on the edge of the sea."

"Where — is — he — now?" the Duke enquired.

"He has left to go to the nearest fishing-village to arrange,

as soon as it is daylight and the sea has subsided, for somebody to row to the yacht and tell them to join me here. It is
very kind of him to do this."

"Very — kind!" the Duke agreed. "But — you are all —
right?"

"I was not hurt. Fortunately, we were very near the shore.
I was only afraid for you."

"The boom hit my head."

"Yes, I know. It knocked you unconscious," Anoushka
said, "but there is nothing broken. The Doctor felt you over
very carefully and said that although your head will ache for
a day or so, you are very strong."

The Duke tried to sit up but found that it hurt him.

"No, lie still," Anoushka instructed, putting out her hand
to prevent him from moving.

As she did so, the Duke saw to his surprise that she was
wearing a man's shirt with the sleeves rolled up.

She gave a little laugh.

"Please . . . do not look at me . . . but as we were both
soaked to the skin, the Doctor insisted that while he un-
dressed you, I should undress too. Our clothes are drying,
and although they will look a mess, we will be able to put
them on in the morning."

"You are quite certain you are not hurt?" the Duke asked.

He spoke automatically, thinking as he did so how beautiful she looked with her hair falling over her shoulders, and
the cotton shirt she was wearing open almost to her waist.

As she was kneeling he could not see how long the skirt
was, but he had the feeling that when she did rise he would
see her legs.

Once again Anoushka read his thoughts.

"I have only just changed after the Doctor left," she said.
"I tried to find a robe or something to make me more
respectable. I have been wringing out my gown, for the
moment it is nothing but a wet rag."

"I am not complaining," the Duke said with a smile. "But I

gather your Doctor friend has not provided me with anything?"

"We were lucky he was there," Anoushka said. "I should
never have been able to carry you from the water, and
certainly not undress you."

She spoke without any shyness and there was only laughter in her voice as she added:

"My instructions are to keep the fire going all night and
see that you rest. If you are hungry there is some food and
of course tea. What Russian would be without his tea?"

"I should like some tea," the Duke said.

He realised that they were in a little wooden hut and he
knew it was just the type of place in which a professional
man would wish to spend his holidays, presuming he had no
wife or children.

It consisted of one room with a large fireplace that burnt
logs, and a bed which was little more than several mattresses
which were pulled close to the fire.

It was quite a large bed, with room for two people, and
the Duke thought that if the Doctor was unmarried he
doubtless, like all Russians, often had a companion to share
his bed.

There were two chairs and a deal-table against one wall,
and a dresser hung with cooking-utensils as well as having
shelves for plates and cups.

On one wall there was a gun, along with several fishing-
rods and a telescope.

Everything was scrupulously clean and tidy.

Anoushka, who was watching the reaction in his eyes,
gave a little laugh.

"It is not as grand as your house in the Champs Élysées or
your Villa in Nice," she said, "but I do not think I have ever
been so glad of a roof over our heads when the Doctor
fished us out of the water."

"I am indeed grateful," the Duke said.

As he spoke, he thought that his luck had not betrayed him.

He had been in some very tight corners in his life and on two occasions he had nearly died, but always he had been saved in the nick of time. Always it appeared that Providence or Fate was on his side, or his proverbial good luck saw him through.

He could imagine what would have happened if their rescuer had not been there. Even if they had not drowned, they might have had to spend a night cold and wet, which might easily have resulted in their developing pneumonia.

"Thank God for my luck!" the Duke said to himself.

It was very nearly a prayer, because he was not thinking of himself but of Anoushka.

"I will make your tea," she said, "and now you will see for yourself that I have thin legs!"

The Duke laughed.

"It is something I have been looking forward to."

She got up without any self-consciousness and he saw that the shirt she was wearing, which obviously belonged to a tall man, reached below her knees.

She had it tied round her waist with what he thought was a man's tie, and with her hair hanging a long way down her back, and her very slim figure, the Duke thought she looked very beautiful, though not in the least like a Lady of Quality or even an alluring woman.

Instead she seemed like some sprite who might have come from the Russian woods or even from the sea.

Only as she busied herself with the samovar did he catch a glance of her large eyes, and once again he was aware that she was more like a goddess from mythology than anything else.

The bed was warm and comfortable, the top mattress and the pillows being filled with goose-feathers, and the Duke, realising that the bruise on his head was not now as painful as it had been, watched his wife brewing the tea.

He knew that it was something she must have done in the
past, for the samovar presented no difficulties.

"Are you hungry?" she asked.

"Not at the moment," the Duke replied, "only thirsty, as I
suspect you are."

"I am looking forward to drinking this tea."

"It is something you have not done since you were eight,"
he remarked.

She did not reply, but she flashed him a glance that was
somehow mischievous, as if she deliberately wanted him to
be curious.

Then she brought two cups from the dresser, filled them,
and sat on the side of the bed.

"How long will our host be away?" the Duke asked.

"He said it was quite a long walk to the fishing-village,"
Anoushka replied, "and he will not attempt to return until
tomorrow morning, when he will bring us some more
food."

"That is very obliging of him," the Duke commented.

"He is such a kind man. He told me he comes from
Odessa and has such a big practice that he finds it difficult to
get away from his work."

"It was fortunate that you could converse with him."

Anoushka looked at the Duke sharply. Then she
laughed.

"You heard me speaking Russian?"

"Yes."

"Were you surprised?"

"With a name like Anoushka, it is a language you should
be able to speak."

"Yes . . . of course."

She turned away to look at the fire, and he did not press
her. He was content just to lie there, feeling the warm tea
seep down through him and watching the flames flicker on
the silver of her hair and the contours of her face.

"I have seen you in many different guises," he said at

length. "As a Novice, as a bride, as a Lady of Fashion in Paris, and now as a peasant in Russia."

"If I am poorly dressed, what about yourself, Your Grace?"

"What could I be but Adam in a Garden of Eden alone with Eve?" the Duke replied.

Anoushka's laughter rang out. Then she said:

"You always have an answer. You are so clever, which makes it fascinating to be with you, because I can never guess what you are going to say next."

"That is exactly what I find about you," the Duke said, "and, as you say, it is very fascinating."

As he spoke he gave a little yawn, knowing that while he wanted to talk to Anoushka, the tea and the warm fire made him feel very sleepy.

Anoushka took his empty cup from him.

"You must go to sleep," she said. "The Doctor said you must rest, and it is important that you do so."

"I am tired," the Duke admitted.

"Then sleep," Anoushka said.

She put down the cup, and as he shut his eyes he felt her fingers soothing his forehead, moving over it in a manner which seemed mesmeric.

As she did so, he thought it was the first time she had touched him, and while he tried to think how significant this was, and thrilled to her touch, the world seemed to slip away from him and he was conscious only of the softness of her fingers before he fell asleep . . .

*

The Duke awoke and was aware that everything was very silent.

He thought, although he was not sure, that before he went to sleep there had been a lighted candle on the table.

Now there was only the light of the fire. There was no fear

that it might go out, for there were huge logs on it which had not yet even begun to burn through.

The Duke looked for Anoushka, but at first he could not see her. Then he realised that she was beside him in the bed, with her head on another pillow, and was sound asleep.

For the moment he was astonished. Then he realised that it was the obvious and sensible thing to do, and he was only surprised that she had accepted it as such.

There was nowhere else she could have slept, except on a hard upright wooden chair, and because the bed was large and he was on the side of it nearest to the fire, there was quite a gap between them.

The Duke turned over cautiously so that he could lie on his side and look at Anoushka.

She looked very young when she was asleep, her eyelashes were dark against her cheeks, and her hair was tumbled over the pillow and over her shoulders.

She was still wearing the shirt which the Doctor had provided for her. Her arms were bare, and one of them with its long slim fingers lay outside the blankets.

The Duke looked at her for a long time, then because he could not help himself, because everything seemed far away in another world and of no consequence, he raised himself towards her.

Very gently, almost as if he were kissing a child, his lips touched Anoushka's.

Chapter Seven

HER lips were very soft, sweet, and innocent, and while the Duke meant to be very gentle he could not help increasing the pressure of his mouth until he felt Anoushka stir and she opened her eyes.

"I was ... dreaming about ... you," she murmured drowsily, and he knew she did not realise what was happening.

"I cannot help kissing you," he said, "because it is something I have wanted to do for a long time."

Then he was kissing her again, kissing her insistently, demandingly, and at the same time tenderly.

He realised that she was still half-asleep, but instinctively her body moved towards him, his arms went round her, and he was holding her close against him as he kept her mouth captive.

As he did so, he realised that never in his whole life had he felt such a strange, ecstatic joy in kissing a woman.

While physically he was aroused, he knew there was something spiritual in his love, which he had never known before.

He wanted Anoushka as a woman, but at the same time he felt a reverence for her. He wanted to protect her, fight for her, and prevent her from ever coming in contact with anything that was ugly or wicked, wrong or disturbing.

It was difficult to put his feelings into words, and yet he knew he held something in his arms so perfect, so unspoilt, that he would fight with every fibre of his being to prevent her from being changed or shocked by the world into which he had taken her.

Even as he kissed her he knew with some part of his mind that she had got into bed beside him quite naturally, since it was the only place to sleep.

It had never struck her because she had no idea what a man could feel for a woman, or indeed a woman for a man, that there was anything embarrassing in being next to him.

This was the real purity which he had sought — the purity not only of the body but of the mind.

Then as he raised his head to look down at her, he saw that Anoushka's eyes were wide open, and she said in a whisper:

"I . . . I did not . . . know that . . . being kissed was . . . like that."

"Like what?" the Duke asked, and his voice was deep and a little unsteady.

"Like the . . . feeling I have when I am . . . praying."

"I love you, Anoushka!" the Duke said. "I have tried to prevent myself from telling you so until you loved me, but now that you are beside me I cannot help kissing you."

There was a note of anxiety in his voice as he added:

"You told me you do not like being touched, but, my darling, you have made it impossible for me not to do so."

She smiled and he felt as if a ray of sunshine filled the small hut.

"I like your touching me," she said simply, "and I would like you to kiss me again."

The Duke's arms tightened. Then when his lips were very near to hers he said:

"Tell me, my precious, what you feel about me. I have been patiently waiting — and it has been more difficult than I can ever tell you — for you to love me as a man."

"I do not . . . know what people feel when they are in . . . love," Anoushka replied, "but every day being with you has been like being taken up to Heaven, and every night . . . although I did not tell you so . . . you were in my dreams."

"Why did you not tell me?" the Duke asked.

"Because I did not know you loved me, and I thought because you had been hurt and wounded by some woman it had made it difficult for you to love anybody again."

"I love you!" the Duke said. "I love you as I have never loved before, but I was stupid enough not to guess you were somewhere in the world if only I could find you."

"Do you really . . . mean I am . . . different?"

"Very, very different," the Duke said, "so different, my lovely one, that is is going to take me a lifetime to make you realise how happy we shall be and how different you are in every way from any other woman I have ever known."

He smiled as he added:

"Up until now I have been your teacher. Now I am ready to become your pupil, and you can teach me about the love you feel for me, which you say is part of Heaven."

He did not wait for her answer, but his lips came down on hers and he kissed her until he felt her body quiver against his and knew that the fire that burnt in him had ignited a little flame in her.

But while his heart was beating frantically and his whole body throbbed with desire, the Duke remembered his promise to his sister, and he knew that because he had given her his word he could not break it.

He raised his head and as he did so one of the logs fell lower in the fire.

The flames leapt higher and by the light of them he could see Anoushka's face very clearly.

He stared at her, and he saw in the expression in her eyes the look he had longed to see, and knew that at last, after a wait of what seemed to him a century of time, she was awakening to love.

He realised too that her lips were parted and her breath was coming fitfully through them, and her breasts were moving beneath the thin cotton shirt.

Very gently, so as not to frighten her, he drew it away

from one shoulder, then he was kissing her neck, the white skin of her chest, and the softness of her breast.

He knew as he did so that she was experiencing sensations she had never known existed, and when he looked down at her again she said:

"Love is . . . very exciting . . . why did nobody . . . tell me it was . . . like this?"

"What do you feel?" the Duke asked.

"As if the stars are all glittering in my heart," she said, "and little waves are running through my body, which makes me feel restless and at the same time very . . . very excited."

"And what do you want when you are excited?" the Duke asked.

"I want you to kiss me, and I want to be very . . . very close to you . . . closer and closer so that . . . as the Bishop said when we were married . . . we are really . . . one person."

The Duke knew she did not really understand what she was asking, but was only expressing desire in the most beautiful words he had ever heard said, which made him feel that he too had the stars glittering in his heart.

"I love you! I worship you!" he said. "At the same time, my darling, I cannot make you mine until you ask me to do so."

Anoushka looked puzzled.

"What have I to ask you?"

"When I took you from the Convent," the Duke replied, "because my sister wanted us to find the love she had known before she took her vows, she made me promise that while I made you my wife in name, I would not make love to you completely for three months or until you asked me to do so."

"I do not understand," she answered. "Do you mean that I can be nearer to you . . . than I am now . . . and there is more to . . . making love than just kissing?"

"Much, much more," the Duke said in a deep voice.

"And I can . . . ask you to do . . . that?"

"If you want me to."

She gave a little laugh and he thought that only she could have laughed at this particular moment.

"Of course I want you to love me," she said. "Please . . . please . . . teach me about love . . . the love that will make me your real . . . wife, and we shall be really . . . one person."

There was a touch of passion in Anoushka's voice that had never been there before.

As the Duke kissed away the last words, he felt as if the stars fell from the sky to envelop them, and the love that they felt for each other carried them into a Garden of Eden where they were alone and there was nothing else in the whole Universe but themselves and their love.

*

The Duke woke and realised it was dawn.

The light was coming between the wooden shutters which covered the small windows of the hut.

The fire had burnt down to smouldering ashes, but it was warm and he knew now that the storm had passed and it would undoubtedly be a very hot day.

Then he was aware that Anoushka was cuddled up against him, her head on his shoulder, her hair falling over his arm.

He looked down at her and knew it was impossible for any man to be happier than he was.

Last night when he had made her his, he was aware that they had both touched the peaks of ecstasy, which, with all his experience, he had not known existed.

He had tried to be very gentle with her, but they had been transported out of themselves into a rapture in which there was neither time nor space and they were blinded by the wonder of it.

Only very much later, when he was able to think coherently, did the Duke ask:

"My precious, my darling, I have not hurt you?"

"I love . . . you," Anoushka said. "I love you . . . I love you . . . and I want to go on saying so over and over again because it is . . . so glorious and even to speak the words is like hearing music."

"That is what I thought too," the Duke said, "and, my precious, I am very grateful to be alive and even more grateful to be here alone with you."

He kissed her hair before he said:

"But I never imagined that I would make love to you for the first time in a wooden hut and with only blankets on the bed."

"Does it matter?" Anoushka asked. "To me it is the most glorious place in the world! Perhaps it is a little Planet all by itself, to which we have managed to — fly, and which therefore belongs only to us."

The Duke smiled.

He was thinking of how his sister had said that to step outside the Convent would be for Anoushka to find herself on another Planet.

"All I know is," he said aloud, "that because we are here I not prevent myself from telling you of my love, although it was something which was bound to happen sooner or later."

"I am glad it was sooner," Anoushka said, moving a little nearer to him, "otherwise there might have been more days and weeks when you did not kiss me, and I should never have known how wonderful your kisses could be."

"And when I made love to you? the Duke asked.

"I have no way to explain that," she replied. "I only know that I became one with you and you were not a man but a god from Olympus, or perhaps an Archangel. Now I really belong to you and nobody can . . . take me from . . . you?"

The last words were a question and the Duke's arms suddenly tightened round her as he said fiercely:

"I would kill anybody who tried to! You are mine,
Anoushka! Mine, now and for eternity, and I will never lose
you!"

"That is what I want you to . . . say."

She looked up at him, and while there was a smile on her
lips, there was a touch of anxiety in her strange eyes as she
said:

"You told me I should feel jealous of you . . . but I did not
. . . understand . . . Now I do. If you loved . . . anybody else
but me . . . I think I should want to die!"

"You need not be afraid of that," the Duke said. "I have
never really loved anybody but you. Like you, I had no idea
what real love was like, until last night. Now I know that in
the past I was accepting second-best, my beautiful darling,
and it is something I shall never do again."

Anoushka put her small hand on his chest.

"How can you be so wonderful? she asked. "How can
there be a man in the world like you, who loves me?"

"You have not met many man, my darling," the Duke
said, "but even if you had, I should still want you to think I
am unique."

"But you are," she said, "because I think when God made
us He intended us for each other . . . or is that . . . presumptuous of me?"

"It is what you should think," the Duke said firmly, "and
what I think too. We were made for each other, Anoushka,
and I can only be very, very grateful that I have found you."

Anoushka gave a little cry.

"Supposing you had not come to the Convent? Supposing
you had married somebody else?"

The Duke had a fleeting thought of Cleodel and realised
that now she was no more than a ghost in his life and he
could hardly remember what she looked like.

"We should have trusted Fate," he said, "knowing that
there is a Power that shapes our lives."

He spoke sincerely and thought it was something he would never have said a little while ago.

He had thought himself so self-sufficient, so much the Captain of his own destiny.

Now he knew that the Power of which he had spoken had saved him from the destruction of a marriage which was based on deception and trickery, and had taken him, in his thirst for revenge, to the Convent where he had found Anoushka.

He turned round so that he could hold her closer to him.

"We are neither of us going to look back on the past," he said. "I have done many things, my darling, which I have no wish to discuss with you, and which I do not wish you to know about. All I want to think of is the future — our future together."

"That is what I want, too," Anoushka answered, "and I will try every second, every minute, and every hour of every day to make you happy."

She lifted her lips to his as she spoke and as the Duke kissed her he felt once again the fires of love burning within them, and at the same time they were sanctified by a belief in the power of God that had never been there before.

Anoushka was his, with her body, her heart, and her mind. He knew as he made love to her that their souls were, in a way he could not explain, part of the Divine which had brought them together.

*

The sun was shining brilliantly when the Duke finally opened the shutters and the door of the hut.

Wearing a shirt that belonged to the Doctor and a pair of trousers that were too long for him, he thought the world seemed to glow with a light that came both from himself and from Anoushka.

She was wearing the same shirt that she had worn during the night and her hair fell silkily over it.

As she set the plates and cups on the table and found the food which the Doctor had told her they could eat, she looked very alluring.

Their own clothes were nearly dry, but the Duke said they should lay them out in the sun before they put them on.

"When we have had breakfast," he said, "I am going to swim in the sea."

"You are quite certain the exercise will not make your head ache?" Anoushka enquired.

"I have forgotten about my head," the Duke said. "I think loving you, my darling, is more efficacious than any cure the Doctor could prescribe!"

Anoushka laughed before she said:

"You can always suggest he try it on his other patients!"

The Duke turned from the open door to walk towards Anoushka and take her in his arms.

"Every time I look at you," he said, "you are lovelier than you were a moment before. I think it would be a mistake to waste time and money going back to civilisation. Let us live here for the rest of our lives, and you can wear what you have on now, although actually I prefer you with nothing!"

She laughed up at him completely unselfconsciously.

"It might be rather cold in the winter," she said. "The Russian winters, even in Odessa, can be very, very cold."

The Duke looked at her.

"Now you are going to tell me your secret?" he asked.

"Not at this moment," she replied. "I think you had a reason for bringing me to Odessa, and that is where I will tell you what I have never told anyone else."

"You shall have it your way, my darling one," the Duke said, and kissed her, at first gently, then with a fierce, demanding passion which seemed part of the sun.

*

It was the following morning before the yacht steamed into Odessa Harbour.

The Doctor had kept his word and sent fishermen to tell the yacht where they were, and it had actually arrived in the little bay near the hut at four o'clock in the afternoon.

The Doctor himself had reached them about midday, and after they had thanked him he had gone fishing and once again they were alone in the hut.

"I am so happy . . . I do not want to be . . . rescued," Anoushka said.

"Nor do I," the Duke replied.

He shut the door and bolted it, then carried her back to bed, and it was several hours later when they looked out to sea and saw the yacht steaming down the coast towards them.

The Duke had never seen Odessa before, but it was just as he had expected it to be.

Beyond the harbour, which was beautiful, he could see a great number of turrets and towers of the buildings which he knew from his study of Russia had been built by Prince Voronzov when he had become Governor-General of New Russia and Bessarabia.

Under his guidance, the land round Odessa had flourished.

The Duke was interested in seeing what he had read about the city. At the same time, it was difficult to think of anything but Anoushka.

He knew by the way her eyes shone that she was excited, and yet when she slipped her hand into his he knew she was also apprehensive.

He had already found that she had endearing little gestures that he had never expected before, after growing used to her serenity and her innocently impersonal ways.

As his fingers closed tightly over hers he felt everything she did, and everything she said brought him a new happiness, and he had never known that he could feel so different or so complete as a man.

He knew that he still had a great deal to teach her about

love and that she was like the bud of a flower, its petals just opening to the sunshine.

The fact that he was the sun to Anoushka made him feel proud and yet at the same time humble as he had never humbled himself in the past.

"I love you!" he said to her a hundred times.

Yet he knew that words were inadequate to express the breadth and depth of his love, which grew every minute that he was with her.

The gang-plank was let down and the Duke saw one of the stewards hurry onto the quay.

He had been told to procure for them a *troika* to carry them to where Anoushka wished to go, and a few minutes later they saw one coming towards the ship.

It was drawn by three horses and was painted and carved in a very attractive manner.

The coachman, with long hair and a moustache and beard, swept his strangely shaped cap from his head with a courteous gesture as Anoushka explained to him in Russian where they wished to go.

She did not tell the Duke where she was taking him, but as the horses started off at what seemed a tremendous pace, she put her arm into his and said:

"This is something I never dreamt would happen."

"That you would come back here?" he asked.

"That I should be able to do so without being afraid."

"Afraid?" he questioned.

"No-one can hurt me now that I am your wife, can they?"

"No-one!" the Duke said firmly.

He laid his hand on hers and said:

"I knew last night, when we loved each other, that I would protect and fight for you and not allow anything or anybody ever to frighten you."

"I knew you felt like that," she said simply, "and it makes me feel different from the way I have felt all these years."

The Duke did not ask for an explanation. They were now

climbing away from the lower part of the town where the harbour was situated, to where high on the cliffs which rose sheer above the sea there were the beautiful buildings which had been erected by Prince Voronzov.

They passed the Palace, then came to another very fine building, and the expression on Anoushka's face told the Duke that it meant something personal to her.

The *troika* stopped and they both got out. He thought she would go to the front of the building, but instead she led the way to one side of it, and the Duke realised it was a Chapel.

It was very ornately built and, in Russian-fashion, was painted in brilliant colours with a gold dome shining brilliantly in the sun.

The Duke opened the door and there was the scent of incense, and he saw that while the Chapel was not very large it was very beautiful.

There were Ikons on the walls, silver lamps hanging from the ceiling, and there were flowers, candles, and an inescapable atmosphere of sanctity.

Anoushka walked up the aisle and as the Duke followed her he saw that kneeling ahead at the Sanctuary was a Priest.

He was obviously deep in prayer, and as Anoushka stood still as if waiting for him, the Duke also waited, watching her.

Then, as if Anoushka's presence communicated itself to the Priest, he rose to his feet and turned round.

For one moment Anoushka was still, then she ran forward to kneel in front of him.

The Priest spoke and the Duke fancied it was a question, as if he asked what she needed.

Then she looked up at him from her knees and said in Russian:

"You do not recognise me, *Mon Père,* which is not surprising."

The Priest looked around and the Duke saw that he was a

very old man and his hair was white, and he thought perhaps he had difficulty in seeing clearly.

Then he exclaimed, also speaking first in Russian and then in French:

"It cannot be — but it is! Anoushka! *Ma petite!* You are really here?"

"I am really here, *Mon Père*, and I have brought my husband to meet you."

"Your husband!" the Priest exclaimed.

Anoushka rose, and as the Duke came forward she said:

"This is Father Alexis, who baptised me when I was born, instructed me in my faith, and taught me my lessons before I went to the Convent."

The Duke held out his hand and the Priest bowed over it.

"I am the Duke of Ravenstock, Father," he said, "and, as Anoushka has told you, we are married."

"I pray you will both be very happy," the Priest answered, "and you must tell me all about it, my children. Come with me."

He led the way out by another door and they found themselves in a cloister.

The Priest took them through a door which led into what the Duke was sure was his own private house.

It was small, austere, but at the same time beautiful, and he led them into a room where while the furniture was sparse the walls were decorated with very fine Ikons.

Anoushka gave a cry of delight.

"This is where I came for my lessons, and only when I reached the Convent did I realise how well you had taught me."

The Priest smiled.

"I am glad about that, but let me look at you, Anoushka. You were a pretty child, but you have grown into a very beautiful woman."

Anoushka did not reply. She merely looked at the Priest

as if she wanted him to say more, and, as if he understood, he added:

"You are very like your mother."

"That is what I wanted you to say!" Anoushka exclaimed. "But I think I have also a resemblance to Papa."

"How, when you were loved so much, could you be anything but like them both?" the Priest asked. "But you must sit down."

With his hand he indicated two chairs near each other, and when they had seated themselves he said:

"I am not surprised that you have married. I always felt somehow that you would not take the veil, and if it was God's will He would provide you with a very different life from that of a Nun."

"God has been very, very kind to me," Anoushka said. "And now, please, as I have kept the secret of Papa and Mama all these years, will you tell my husband what happened, because, as you can imagine, he is very curious."

The Priest smiled.

"That is not surprising, and although you were very young, Anoushka, you were wise beyond your years, and I knew you would never betray your father or do anything which might constitute a danger to him."

"It was not difficult to keep it a secret until I was married," Anoushka said.

She gave the Duke an understanding little smile as she spoke, and he said:

"I am very anxious to hear what this momentous secret is."

"Let me start at the beginning," the Priest said. "Anoushka's mother was born in 1830 and she was a niece of Tsar Nicholas."

"His niece?" the Duke murmured, realising the importance of her position.

"Her Serene Highness Princess Natasha," the Priest went

on, "was born into a position of luxury and importance that I am sure I need not describe to Your Grace."

The Duke inclined his head to show that he understood, and the Priest went on:

"As she grew up, Her Serene Highness was very different from the other pleasure-loving Royalty at the Court of St. Petersburg. When she was twenty it was decided that she should marry, and a husband was chosen for her without her being consulted, which I am sure Your Grace will understand is traditional."

"Of course," the Duke agreed.

"The Princess, however, was appalled by the suffering of the Serfs and the poorer citizens of St. Petersburg, and, disliking the man who had been chosen as her husband, she decided to withdraw from the world and enter a Convent."

The Duke was listening intently but he did not interrupt, and the Priest continued:

"Because she thought nobody would listen to her while she remained at Court, Her Serene Highness ran away before anybody could stop her and travelled to Odessa, where her father had a Palace he never used and which had over the years fallen into disrepair.

"When the Princess arrived, she was so beautiful, so young, and so full of life that I told her I thought it was a mistake for her to withdraw from the world and she should think over seriously what she was about to do, before she finally committed herself."

The Priest smiled at Anoushka before he said:

"As perhaps you will remember, my child, your mother was a very determined person, and she told me she had made up her mind. I think she was also afraid that if she did not do something quickly, the Tsar would have her brought back to St. Petersburg."

"It was the Tsar Nicholas at that time," the Duke interposed.

"It was indeed, Your Grace, a cruel, wicked tyrant whose

crimes have left an indelible mark on the history of our country."

As the Priest spoke he crossed himself, then continued:

"The Tsar sent members of the Secret Police to Odessa, but by that time the Princess had taken her vows in the small community of working Nuns, and I was able to send them away, saying that Her Serene Highness now belonged to God, and even the Tsar had no jurisdiction over her."

The Priest paused before he said:

"This, God forgive me, was not quite true. When I had accepted Her Serene Highness into the Church, I had made her submission to her vows revocable so that if at any time she wished to do so she could return to the world."

"But the Tsar was not aware of it?"

"No one was aware except myself," the Priest answered, "and of course the Princess."

There was silence for a moment as he thought back into the past. Then he said:

"After a few years the small community of Nuns moved from the very inadequate and uncomfortable house which was their Convent into the Palace. This was after Her Serene Highness's father had died, and he had left her the Palace in his Will."

"So the Palace became a Convent," the Duke said.

"Exactly," the Priest agreed, "and it was more convenient for me and for them. We also had room for a Hospital, which we arranged in one wing of the Palace."

"They were Nursing Nuns?"

"All of them," the Priest said, "and they are the only Nurses to be found in the whole of Southern Russia. Our Doctors are very grateful to have them, I can assure you."

The Duke knew it was very rare for women to be Nurses either in peace or in war, and he knew, having served as a soldier, how inadequate the military Doctors and orderlies were and that the troops more often died from lack of attention than at the hands of their enemies.

"Everything was peaceful and uneventful," the Priest went on, "until 1865, when Sir Reginald Sheridan came to Odessa."

"Papa!" Anoushka exclaimed.

"Your father," the Priest agreed. "He had been a great traveller, having been round the world several times, but the strain of the journeys had proved too much for his health, and he bought a house on the outskirts of the city, intending to write a book on his journeys and also to spend the rest of his life in a climate that suited him."

"I seem to remember an author by that name," the Duke said.

"I have copies of the three books he wrote," the Priest replied, "and I will give them to Your Grace."

"Thank you."

"Sir Reginald was not only a very distinguished man but also an extremely interesting one, and we became, I am honoured to admit, friends," the Priest said. "Then the second winter he was here he became seriously ill."

The Duke felt he already knew the end of the story.

"He was so ill," the Priest continued, "that, thinking he was dying, Her Serene Highness had him moved into the Convent, or Palace, whichever you like to call it, where he had a quiet room overlooking the garden and the sea, where we expected him to breathe his last."

"But he lived!" Anoushka cried in a rapt voice.

"He lived entirely owing to your mother's ministrations," the Priest answered, "and while she nursed him they fell in love."

The old man spoke quite simply. Then he went on:

"They had found a happiness together that could only have come from God, and they asked me what they should do about it."

"And what did you reply?" the Duke enquired.

"I married them," the Priest said simply. "It had of course to be a very secret marriage, because if the Tsar had learnt what had happened — even though he was not now the cruel Nicholas but Tsar Alexander II — Her Serene Highness's alliance, even with someone so highly distinguished as Sir Reginald, would not have been permitted."

"I can understand that," the Duke said.

The Priest sighed.

"I do not think I have ever known two people so happy, and it was easy for them to keep their secret when everyone thought Sir Reginald was still too ill to go back to his own house, and your mother was now the Mother Superior. They could therefore be alone without anybody else being aware of it."

"I can understand now," Anoushka said in a very low voice, "as I have never been able to do before, why they were so happy."

She looked at the Duke as she spoke, and he knew she was thinking of the rapture and ecstasy they had found together in the little hut.

He smiled at her, then forced himself to listen again to the Priest.

"Your father and mother were rapturously happy," the old man was saying, "until several years later when Her Serene Highness discovered she was with child."

"How old was she?" the Duke asked.

"She was within a month of her fortieth birthday, so it was something neither she nor Sir Reginald had any idea might happen."

"What did she do?"

Because of the white robes Her Serene Highness wore, it was quite easy to conceal her condition until it was nearing the time for her baby to be born."

The Priest was silent for a moment, as if he was remembering the long discussions there must have been between the three of them.

"What did you do?" the Duke asked, as if he could hardly bear the suspense of not knowing.

"We announced that the Doctor who was attending Sir Reginald wished him to go to Constantinople for a second medical opinion on his condition. Of course, he was too ill to travel alone and was therefore accompanied by the Reverend Mother, and her maid, who was an elderly woman utterly devoted to her and who she would have trusted with her life."

"So Anoushka was born in Constantinople," the Duke said.

"I wish I could remember it," Anoushka said with a sigh.

"You were born," the Priest replied, "and three weeks later Sir Reginald with Her Serene Highness returned with you to Odessa."

"How did you explain the new additon to the Convent?" the Duke asked.

"I am afraid that to make the story of Anoushka's appearance convincing, we had to tell a number of lies," the Priest answered, "for which I did many long penances,"

"What was your explanation?" the Duke enquired.

"Sir Riginald announced that when he was in Constantinople he had found a distant relative who had just given birth to a child. She had been recently widowed and she had not enough money to return home before the baby was born. Unfortunately, while the baby survived, she died."

"Very ingenious."

"To make it sound more convincing," the Priest went on, "Sir Reginald announced that he had adopted the child as his own, and, when she could speak, Anoushka called him 'Papa'."

"I loved Papa," Anoushka said, "and although nobody told me he had died, I knew it before my husband informed me that he had left me all his money."

"How did you know?" the Duke asked.

"It is difficult to explain," Anoushka replied. "I felt a sudden sense of loss, and when I was praying in the Chapel I suddenly felt him near me, so near me that I knew that it was true and he was no longer in Odessa, but in another world from which he could reach me."

"You were blessed, my child, by his presence," the Priest said, "and I know that because his thoughts were always with you, if he was able to do so he would come to you and be as near as he was permitted to be."

What I cannot understand," the Duke said, "is why Sir Reginald sent her away."

"I am just coming to that, Your Grace. Her Serene Highness died unexpectedly when Anoushka was only eight years old. I think perhaps because she was older than the average when Anoushka was born, and the Doctor who attended her in Constantipole was not very skilful, she often suffered pains which she would not admit. She grew very thin and found it difficult to eat."

"I did not know this!" Anoushka cried.

"Nor did your father." the Priest said. "She was so happy with you both that she would never have allowed there to be a cloud in your sky. But I had known for a long time that she was not as well as she should be. Nevertheless, when she died it was a great shock."

"I can remember it!" Anoushka said in a whisper.

Because she sounded so unhappy, the Duke took her hand in his, and as if the touch of him comforted her she moved her chair a little nearer to his and held on to him almost as if she felt he was a lifeline, and she would not let go.

"It was then that I realised the full impact of Her Serene Highness's death," the Priest said, "and I knew it would be dangerous for Anoushka to stay here."

"Dangerous?" the Duke asked.

"I had to inform the Tsar in St. Petersburg that a member of his family had died, and I knew that the moment the news reached him, not only Court Officials but the Secret Police would descend on us to make enquiries as to the cause of Her Serene Highness's death. We had thought that living here, at what seemed like the end of the world, we were safe from gossip and the tongues of those who are always ready to make trouble."

"What did you do?"

"The important thing of which both Sir Reginald and I were aware was that, whoever her father might be, Anoushka was in fact Royal, the grandchild of an Arch-Duke, a cousin of the reigning Tsar."

"You mean they might have taken her away?"

"Most certainly they would have done so," the Priest replied. "She would have been taken to St. Petersburg and brought up in the life from which her mother had fled."

"Now I understand," the Duke said.

"I thought you would," the Priest answered. "That was why, even though it was a great wrench, Sir Reginald, thinking only of Anoushka, took her to France."

"You knew about the Convent of the *Sacré-Coeur* where my sister is the Mother Superior?" the Duke asked.

"I had heard of it through a Catholic Priest with whom I had a lifelong correspondence, and Sir Reginald knew Your Grace's family and had met some members of it."

"But it was your idea that Anoushka should go to France?"

"It was my idea, and Sir Reginald agreed that it would be the best and safest place for her."

"It was very hard to say good-bye to Papa," Anoushka said.

"I can understand that," the Duke agreed, "but he was saving you from a very much worse life. I do not think you would have been happy in St. Petersburg."

"Mama always spoke of it with horror," Anoushka answered, "and I knew she was frightened of the Secret Police."

"There is no-one in Russia who is not frightened of them even now," the Priest said, "and although things are better, it would be a mistake, Your Grace, for anybody here to know of Anoushka's real identity."

"I agree with you," the Duke said, "and I promise you that as far as I am concerned nobody will ever be aware of Anoushka's Russian origins, altough I imagine there would be no reason, now that her father is dead, for not saying she was his child."

"Not in England, at any rate," the Priest said, "but I would rather you did not speak of it in Odessa."

"I will not do so," the Duke promised. "And now that we have come here and you have told me what I wished to know, I shall take Anoushka away."

He paused before he said quietly:

"Before we leave, I would like to ask you, Father, if you will bless us, because although we were married in a Catholic Church, I think it would make my wife happy to have a special blesssing from you in the Church where she really belongs."

"There is nothing which would make me happier, Your Grace," the Priest replied simply.

As the Duke rose to his feet, Anoushka laid her cheek for a moment against his shoulder and he heard her whisper so that only he could hear:

"You understand! Oh, my darling, wonderful, precious husband, you understand!"

*

After dinner that night, the Duke and Anoushka went out on deck to look at the lights of Odessa.

The yacht was no longer tied to the quay but was anchored at the entrance to the harbour, from where they had a panoramic view of the town, the tall cypress trees, and the undulating country beyond it.

It had been beautiful in the day-time, but now at night it had a mystic glory that was accentuated by the moonlight on the golden domes and the glittering lights in the houses which looked like stars that had fallen down.

The real stars filled the great arc of the Heavens above them, and the moon sent shafts of light glimmering over the waters of the sea, making a picture that the Duke thought he would never forget.

When he realised that Anoushka, standing by his side, was very silent, he turned to look at her, feeling that no beauty, however sensational, could hold him when she was there.

As if she had need of him, because the sight of where she had lived with her father and mother and what she had heard today made her emotional, she moved closer to him and he knew she wanted the comfort and strength of his arms, and he held her close.

"What are you thinking?" he asked in his deep voice.

"That no woman could have a more intriguing and exciting background, but, my darling, although this must be a secret between ourselves, we must never forget."

"I knew you would you feel like that," the Duke said.

"What is so wonderful is that as Papa and Mama loved each other so tremendously . . . I was born of love."

The Duke did not speak, but his lips were on her hair as she went on:

"That is what I want our children to be born of a love as great as theirs and ours, so that they in their turn will be able to give love as I can give it to you."

"And I to you, my precious, adorable little wife."

The Duke looked at the sky for a moment. Then he said, and his voice was very moving:

"I asked for a woman pure and untouched, and that is what I found, but I was also given someone so perfect that I want to fall down on my knees in gratitude."

Anoushka looked up at him, her eyes no longer mysterious but deep and dark with another emotion.

"I am talking about you, my darling, and love," the Duke went on. "To me they are one and the same. I love you until